HAUNTED TALES FROM APPALACHIA

Ghosts, Spirits and Other
Strange Happenings from
the Hills and Hollows

Ashley C. Stinnett

Acknowledgements:

Book Art and Design: Justin Williams

Creative Consultation: Sara Stinnett

Pen & Inkwell Publishing

First Edition.

Printed in the United States of America.

ISBN: 979-8-9883105-0-1

This book is dedicated to my
beautiful family and to all of
the mountain storytellers.

To: LAURA
HOPE YOU ENJOY!
THiS SPOOKY READ!
THANKS FOR BEING
A GREAT FRIEND.
—ASHLEY—

CONTENTS

Introduction 1

Chapter 1: Strange Happenings 7

  1. The Levitating Table 8
  2. Something Is In the Crops 14
  3. The Drifter 20

Chapter 2: The Macabre 25

  4. The Devil Is In The Pudding 26
  5. The Man With Many Faces 34
  6. The Minford Murders 39

Chapter 3: Scary Places 47

  7. McKendree Road Hauntings 48
  8. Pike County Distillery 50
  9. The Allegheny Witch 52

Chapter 4: Hauntings 55

  10. The Haunted Organ 56
  11. They will find you 58
  12. Spoons in the Graveyard 61

Chapter 5: Coal Camp Legends 65

  13. King Solomon's Revenge 66
  14. The Betsy Lane Disaster 69
  15. The Grundy Killer 72

Chapter 6: Supernatural Forces 75

  16. Whitewater Evil 76
  17. The Winds of Whitley 79
  18. Fire on the Mountain 83

Chapter 7: Deadly Dwellings......................87

19. The Legend of Pumpkin Tooth House 88
20. The Strange Picture on the Wall 91
21. A Funhouse to Die For 93

Chapter 8: Mountain Creatures 97

22. The Rusty Shackles 98
23. The Cave Thing 107
24. Someone Lives in the Fog 112

Chapter 9: Creepy Hollows.........................117

25. The Pickety Cemetery...............................118
26. The Path 122
27. The Greenbottom Swamp.............................126

Chapter 10: Holiday Terror 129

28. The Dark Elf of Millersburg........................130
29. All Hallows Evil...................................133
30. A Thanksgiving Carving.............................138

Chapter 11: Spirit Lairs.........................141

31. Big Trouble in Benton 142
32. Dead End Diner 145
33. Funeral Parlor Prank..............................149

Chapter 12: Unexplained Mysteries 155

34. The Coffin in the Creek...........................156
35. The Beech Fork UFO...............................159
36. The Georgia Lake Creature 161

Chapter 13: Treacherous Towns....................167

37. The Cult of Knoxville.............................168
38. The Lynchburg Liar 173
39. Halloween Town of Harrisburg......................178
40. Hillbilly Highway to the Afterlife 185

About the Author 192

WARNING: SPOOKY CONTENT AHEAD

INTRODUCTION

I became fascinated with ghosts and scary stories as a kid. Aside from my love of sports and the outdoors, my early childhood was centered on the paranormal. For years I would watch scary films and read stories, ingesting everything I could from the world of the macabre. To this day, my family still enjoys gathering around to recount a story passed down through the ages. Unfortunately, delving into the world of the supernatural was all fun and games until I reached the age of 12. That is when I would be thrust into a real-life haunting that would nearly take my life.

I remember that bizarre dark spot that appeared over our dining room table that awful year. It had a black soulless look of evil. No matter how many contractors came and repaired our roof that spot never went away. As hard as it was for me to admit at that time, I was terrified of that creepy house. The old remodeled two-story farmhouse my family called "home" was located right on the main highway that runs through my hometown in West Virginia. It had a large front porch, an earthen outdoor cellar and a nice yard. But it was hard to appreciate the positives when you're running around mortified at the thought of having to be stuck home alone. Throughout 1993, my immediate family experienced one strange occurrence after another. I will never forget coming home from school one day and listening to my mother talk about how she came downstairs (from cleaning) to find all of the kitchen cabinets and drawers wide open as if someone had been in the house scavenging for something. Or that time my brother felt someone nudge him over and over while he slept. And each time he woke nobody was there but a swinging mini-blinds string. I vividly remember hating the thought of having to walk up the steps to the second floor because I knew fear would overtake me. Each time I would make the return trip back down, it would always feel like someone was walking up close behind me. Whenever I would have friends over, I could always tell they sensed something was odd about the house. So I knew I wasn't alone in my fear.

During that bizarre summer my brother was home alone. One day he was downstairs listening to his "boom box" when all at once he heard yelling coming from the upstairs part of the house. At the time, he believed it was my mother and our former step-father arguing. So he turned the volume off and listened but there was only silence. He turned the music back on and after a few minutes the yelling began once more. He turned the volume down again only to discover silence. For the third time he turned the music back on, only this time the yelling was even louder. Now, he turned the radio completely off. But this time the yelling didn't stop. In fact, it grew worse and worse. He gradually made his way up the stairs fearing somebody could be in trouble, but suddenly realized that both our mother and stepfather were at work. As he recalls, a chill came over him as if he all at once came to grips with a supernatural presence. As he slowly stopped walking, he could hear what sounded like two adults arguing in un-audible voices that expressed something sinister. The next move my brother made was right out of the door and across the highway to our grandmother's house. In fact, my brother left in such a mad rush that it wasn't until after he got across the street that he realized all he was wearing was a pair of boxer shorts. To this day, I don't believe my brother, who is a career military and law enforcement veteran, ever wanted to be in that house again. Up until that incident, he was a self-proclaimed skeptic towards anything he couldn't physically see or touch. But that house made him a believer in the real possibilities of another world existing beyond our realm.

As each night came and went, I always wondered how things could get worse. Unfortunately, I was about to find out in the early weeks of December. On a cold and rainy night, my mother violently shook me from my deep sleep. When I woke up I could smell fire. The thick black smoke created a fog in our rooms upstairs. As my mother and I felt our way towards the walls, we knew we had to escape in order to survive. The entire first floor was engulfed in flames. I could hear windows exploding as if someone were downstairs emptying one shotgun shell after another. The cracking and popping of wood made me even more scared I would die. As my mom screamed, I began using my fists to punch through thick double-paned windows. We were both able to crawl out onto the roof where we yelled and screamed for anyone who would listen. After what seemed like an eternity, my grandmother eventually ran outside yelling in horror. A few minutes later, her elderly neighbors made an attempt to drag a ladder across the highway to save us. Our problem was we only had two neighbors (counting my grandmother) and both were elderly. As the night dragged on and rain soaked us on that roof, I knew the bottom part of the home was not far from falling in. The popping was getting louder and the fire hotter. I could feel the heat and see the bright flames dancing around underneath our roof. I kept thinking how long that structure would hold up with so much heat covering it. Things got so bad that my mom and I briefly discussed jumping, knowing it would result in severe injuries. As we kept yelling and yelling, I felt a sharp pain shooting through my right hand and leg. I couldn't really see anything due to the lateness of the night and all of the rain pouring over me, so I brushed it off.

Finally, after roughly 25 minutes of being helpless on that roof, we could hear sirens. A few moments more and our long winding gravel driveway was inhabited by firetrucks and ambulances. I'll never forget being carried off that roof. I was drenched, wearing nothing but a pair of soot stained boxer briefs. I remember looking at the house as I was being put into the ambulance. The flames roared throughout where I used to live. It was as if they were on a vengeance.

Later at the hospital, I realized the pain I felt was the openings of skin on my hand and leg. I had slit my right wrist, deeply cut my thumb from top-to-bottom and carved open a gash on my right shin. This was all the result of breaking and crawling through thick farm glass windows to escape the inferno. My guess is, while I was on the roof, I was under so much adrenaline that I didn't have time to stop and focus on my agony. Sadly, the injuries weren't reserved for just me. My mother severely cut her fingers from the broken glass. They were cut so deep that her nerve endings didn't function for years. The flames had burned her hair, eyebrows and eye lashes. This was largely in part to her opening a door that was engulfed in fire from the other side. On top of the cuts, we both suffered from severe smoke inhalation. I remember the tubes down my throat continually sucking soot out of my lungs for hours. The good news was that we were alive. The bad news was our home was completely gutted and we would be wearing hand-me-downs for Christmas. We had lost everything. After a few weeks, the fire department determined that electric wiring had melted in the walls causing a virtually unstoppable interior fire that spread violently fast.

I remember the nurse at the hospital stating how lucky we were to be alive. I also remember being told by one of the fireman that a few seconds later and we would not have survived. In fact, due to the nature of the smoke inhalation, the medical professionals were a little taken aback as to how we woke up in order to escape. To this day, without a blink, my mother says it was her dad waking her up. He had passed away from a heart attack several years prior but she believes she was shoved from the bed moments after the flames began sweeping through the home. The old saying is God has a purpose for each and every one of us. For reasons beyond my thinking, my mother and I were both saved that night. While our faith is strong, we also believe that the warning signs were there. Was our haunting a supernatural entity warning of us of the ensuing fire? Or was our paranormal experience the work of something evil that caused the fire?

For now, we'll never know.

What we do know is; as long as the hills have been around, another dimension has been there. The stories and people you are about to read are fiction, but most of the locations are real. Each tale is designed to take the reader on a journey into a world of the chilling.

Good luck and most importantly, have fun!

Chapter 1

STRANGE HAPPENINGS

1
THE LEVITATING TABLE

The year was 1965 and southern West Virginia was experiencing an unusual heat wave that early November. The trees were beginning to look bare and the clouds seemed to cover the little town of Matewan like a thick grey blanket. The streets were protected by a layer of multi-colored leaves. In some places, the street wasn't even visible to the naked eye. A mere two blocks from Main Street was a small one-story brick home; a leftover remnant from the early turn of the century. One quick glance of the home reveals a lackadaisical approach to repairing anything damaged. The lime-green shutters were as worn out as the partially-caved in front porch. The sidewalk was part concrete and part cinder with hints of grass and weeds popping through. Inside the home was Mary Turner, a soft-spoken, mild-mannered housewife who took pride in her biscuits and gravy recipe. Her husband had died ten years prior from a brief battle with cancer related to his days as a coal miner. Mrs. Turner never remarried out of loyalty. In fact, one could say she was married to her love of cooking. Folks lined up for a mile during the summer to get a taste of her homemade blackberry pie and apple crumb cake. Aside from her love of cooking, Mrs. Turner possessed another unique gift, one of the supernatural realms.

One Thursday evening her twin grandsons had stopped by to enjoy her delicious, warm biscuits and gravy. After dinner the two boys were called into the living room for a "round-table meeting" as she referred to it. Now, typically, after a good meal the boys would either go outside or throw rocks at the train tracks or they would take a short walk down to the store and purchase a candy bar. What else is there for a couple of twelve year old kids to do in a one-horse town? So they gathered around a large round card table with their grandmother for a night they would remember for the rest of their lives.

Mrs. Turner had instructed the boys to sit down facing opposite each other around the table. They both were seated in somewhat corroded fold-out chairs. She then proceeded to spread out an off-white sheet as if not to get the table dirty. She pulled up to the table an old wooden antique styled chair with blue cushions and sat down. She then told the boys to place their hands on the table with their palms facing down. Of course, the boys were curious which led to outbursts of giggling. "Be quiet," she said. "I am going to show you something tonight that my mother and her mother showed all of us a long, long time ago." The boys knew that when grandmother was speaking in a serious tone, it was time for them to get serious as well. She then instructed her grandsons to close their eyes and remain quiet as a mouse for the next few minutes. As the minutes passed, feeling like an eternity, one of the boys slightly opened his eyes to see his grandmother's head was slumped over on the table. Fearing she might be sick, he started to get up. He couldn't move his body at all. It was as if he had been superglued to the chair and his hands had been cemented to the table. All at once the table began to shift left and right, back and forth, ever so gently. The boy wanted to scream but couldn't. He turned to his brother who was staring back at him speechless. The two wanted to say something, anything, but knew their grandmother has instructed them to be quiet at all costs.

Suddenly Mrs. Turner's eyes opened so wide it gave the appearance of a zombie-like trance. "WHERE HAVE YOU GONE," she screamed. The boys, now in a state of complete shock, tried again to get up from the table but couldn't. "HAROLD!" she screamed. "HAROLD...YOU PROMISED ME HAROLD!" She just kept screaming the name of a man the boys had never heard of. All at once the table slowly began rising off of the floor. As the table climbed higher and higher in the air, the older twin was able to belt out, "PLEASE STOP GRANDMA!"

Without hesitation the table quickly dropped. Mrs. Turner's head slumped over on the table and there was dead silence. The boys felt a strange jolt throughout their fingers that traveled down to their toes. It was as if they had just stuck their tongue to the end of a 9-volt battery. They felt their hands being released from the table causing them to quickly spring out of the chairs. They slowly made their way over to their grandmother. "Grandma, are you ok," asked the younger brother. Nothing but silence surrounded them all. Both boys began shaking their grandmother as if to wake her up out of a deep nightmare. But all they heard was silence. As they walked into the kitchen to call for help, they heard a calm voice from the living room. "Boys, come in here so I can finish our talk," Mrs. Tuner softly said. The boys turned to go back into the living room but noticed their grandmother's head was still slumped over on the table. "Why would she be speaking to us like that," the younger brother said. "She isn't being herself." The older brother, as if to be the voice of reason, told his young sibling to stay put while he investigated. Walking slowly towards the card table, he noticed his grandmother barely breathing up and down, up and down. "Grandma, please tell us if you are ok," he said trembling. When he made it over to the table, Mrs. Turner's head began shaking like a dryer full of shoes. The young boy stood in horror, realizing something terrible was happening. "Stay in the kitchen!" he yelled to the younger twin. "Whatever happens, do not come in here." As the eldest sibling slowly reached down to help his grandmother, Mrs. Turner sprung up out of her chair like a force of energy. Her face was ghostly white, her eyes missing, with only charcoal grey sunken hollows in their places. Her hair had turned as black as midnight. Her skin was stretched across a face that appeared to have just lost several pounds of weight. She violently grabbed her grandson's hand like a vice-grip. He tried, but couldn't pull free. As he struggled to get free, she reached her hand out to touch his mouth as if to tell him to shush. She slowly pulled her finger away from his face. The boy's lips were now missing and his eyes were rolled back into his head. As the younger brother began screaming, Mrs. Tuner yelled at the top of her lungs, "I TOLD YOU ALL TO BE QUIET. WE MUST FINISH OUR CHAT," *-

Ten years have passed since those events. After sitting vacant for a while, that old house was finally sold and torn down. Mrs. Turner, who is now in her late eighties, is living her final days out at St. Anthony's, a psychiatric unit located a few miles north of Knoxville, Tennessee. To this day she believes her grandsons will stop by and visit her for some of her famous biscuits and gravy. Unfortunately, the two boys were never found. Several years ago, the police finally stopped searching. The only person who could ever solve the mystery is Mrs. Turner. "Can you bring me my skillet and mixer?" she softly asks the nurse. "Mrs. Tuner, we don't have those for you today, "the nurse says. "But my grandkids will be here this evening. It is Thursday evening isn't it?" she asks. As the nurse turns to leave Mrs. Turner's room, she looks back to see her head slumped over in her hands. It sounds as if she is weeping uncontrollably. "Mrs. Tuner, please get some rest. Tomorrow we will take you for a walk and get you something good to eat," the nurse says to console her. But the sobbing continues.

As the nurse walks over to Mrs. Turner, she notices her hair is now discolored and her hands have gotten considerably paler. "Mrs. Tuner, are you ok?" The nurse gently places her hand on Mrs. Tuner's shoulder. All at once, Mrs. Turner extends her skeletal fingers towards the nurse's mouth. She covers her mouth like a vice-grip. The old woman bolts out of her seat screaming, "I TOLD YOU TO BE QUIET SO WE CAN FINISH OUR CHAT."

2

Something Is In the Crops

Silas Wilbur was a farmer in a quaint southern Pennsylvania town. This little village was known to be a hotbed for tourism. Mr. Wilbur's crops were no less short of remarkable. Each year, he would produce hundreds of bags of potatoes, gallons of raw milk and bushels of vegetables. And every autumn he would make a journey to the local grocer and churches to donate much of what he grew. During the Christmas season, as the snow covered his fields, Silas would turn a portion of his 200 acres into a virtual light orchestra. He is the man many admire; a hard worker of simple upbringings who became wealthy off of his talents. But something was bizarre about Mr. Wilbur's crops during the fall of 1994.

That year was the worst drought experienced in Pennsylvania since records have been kept. In fact, every farmer within a 100 mile radius experienced dried up and decayed fields. Except Mr. Wilbur's fields were plentiful, as if the rain had never ceased. For a half a mile stretch, corn stalks appeared as if they could touch the clouds. Rows upon rows of plump orange round pumpkins lay waiting to be plucked and placed on doorsteps for Halloween. Group after group of potato piles were spread out in endless lines. Amazingly enough, 1994 appeared to be the most productive year yet for Silas Wilbur even though it was one of the worst years for virtually every other farmer in the region. Unfortunately, it only took a few days before the local townsfolk began raising questions.

One day while Mr. Wilbur was busy tending to his corn, Mayor Ferguson stopped by for a visit.

"Good Afternoon Mr. Wilbur, I see you're busy so I won't be here long," the mayor said with a face of reluctant happiness. As the mayor spoke, Silas listened but never looked away from poking and prodding the dirt. "Anyway, I see you are having a good year. You know, most of the other farmers are in for the worst year of their life," he said. Silas slowly raised his head up, looking frustrated while breaking his silence. "Are you asking me to give them some of my crops for free to get through winter?' Silas said with a scowl. The Mayor began fumbling over his words. "Nope, not at all. I was just wondering what your secret was, to...you know...getting so many good crops in such a bad year," he said.

Visibly frustrated, Silas snapped back. "Look, there ain't a secret here. I've been putting in good soil for months. You know this, the whole town knows this. Do you realize how much I have spent to get this right, Mayor? Do you know what I give in charity every single year?

Mayor Ferguson realized the farmer was in no mood for a chat so he quietly gestured and walked off towards his car.

Later that day two college aged students were headed out of town when their car broke down about a quarter of mile from Silas' farm. Unfortunately, after several attempts to reach family and friends, both students soon discovered that they were in one of the worst cellular phone spots in the country. The young men, in a state of panic, began a long trek down the road for some help. As they walked the rural two-lane highway, they came upon an old wooden sign at the end of a very desolate gravel road. The sign read, *"Wilbur Farm: Established 1890"*. The two men decided they would venture out towards the end of the road in the hopes they would find a home for help.

Upon reaching an old farmhouse, both men yelled for anyone who could hear them. "Hello!" they called out. Nothing but the sound of a tractor rumbling could be heard. The college students eventually decided to walk around towards the back of the home in hopes of finding anyone who could help them. They soon discovered a poorly designed rock path that seemed to wind down a steep section of the back yard towards a creek bed. The young men decided to take the journey down the path. Once they reached the creek bed, they could no longer hear the sound of the farm tractor. "Listen man, we aren't getting anywhere. I don't think anyone is on this property and we don't know where that tractor sound is coming from," proclaimed one of the students.

All at once out of nowhere Mr. Wilbur appeared which startled the two young men. "What are you two boys doing on my property?" he asked sternly. Visibly shaken, the two college students began backtracking away from the old man. "Sir, we didn't mean any harm. Our car broke down along the highway and we have no cell phone service so we were wondering......" Mr. Wilbur, who is now visibly aggravated, interrupted the college student. "Listen kid, I don't have time to listen to your story and I ain't a mechanic, so I'll just take you to where a phone is so you can call for help," he snarled.

Mr. Wilbur led the two young men up the path to the back of the home. As they approached an old shoddy screen door, he glared back at them. "My phone is right inside. I don't want any snooping around or any funny business," he said. The two young men nodded in agreement as they walked inside.

The interior of the home was dark and damp as if it had not been kept up for a long time. As the two college students walked into a small cluttered office room, they could hear the sound of crunching beneath their feet. When they looked down, there was no carpet under their shoes; only a floor littered with old corn husks. As they passed by an old kitchen, the smell of burnt coffee permeated throughout the room. A brief glance of the countertops revealed piles and piles of green bean strings and molded pumpkin lids.

As the two men wandered in and out of various rooms, it was becoming more and more clear to them that there was not a phone in the home and the old farmer had disappeared. As they approached an old wooden door, a darkly lit room off to the left caught their attention. A faint sound of bubbling fluid echoed through the hallway. Of course, curiosity mandated they check the room out. As they walked in, they gasped at what they were seeing. All over what appeared to be a wooden floor stained with a dark tar-like substance, were empty bags of miracle grow and fertilizer. Also in the room were four neatly placed rustic looking tables. On top of each table was a giant glass container that was labeled "*Embalming Fluid*". "My God, what is this for?" one of the college students asked in shock. The containers were halfway full of a thick yellow fluid. Two filthy tubes protruded from the sides of the containers like long alien arms. As both young men slowly began backing up, one of them shrieked in terror. Lying in the corner of the room next to a baseboard was a partially decomposed hand. Beside the hand were two IV fluid drip bags that were filled with human blood. "Let's get outta here now!" one of the young men screamed. As the two turned around, there stood the old farmer, wearing a bloody apron and holding two large bagging hooks.

About a week later as Mr. Wilbur was out trimming some brush, the county sheriff pulled up the driveway. He rolled the driver's side window down on his brown Crown Victoria cruiser. "Afternoon, Silas," he said with a smile. Mr. Wilbur looked up and gestured. "Say, can you take a look at something for me?" the sheriff asked. Mr. Wilbur put down his hedge trimmers and walked over to the police car. The sheriff extended his left hand out which held a photograph of two college-aged men. "Have you seen these guys around here by chance? Their parents called a few days ago and reported them missing. We think they may have been traveling down here and their car broke down. But we haven't found them or the car," he inquired. "Nope, can't recall any fellas looking like that around here," Silas remarked. "Ok, well if you happen to see anybody you don't recognize, please call me," the sheriff said. As he began rolling his window up, he stopped halfway. "Say, it looks like your crops are looking even better. Simply amazing and just in time for harvest," the sheriff remarked. "Yep, you could say that I have found a way to make the very best sheriff," Silas said with a grin.

3

THE DRIFTER

Many years ago, near the small town of Whipple, a remote community in Southern West Virginia, there was a long dirt road that slithered through a section of the mountain like a snake. In fact, the desolate thoroughfare was referred to by the locals as Copperhead Ridge Road. It was an ideal spot for anyone who wanted to go muddin' on a four-wheeler or an SUV. It was scenery out of a fairy-tale as hundreds of trees hung over the road providing a year-round shield from the sun. Only when the leaves were gone during the winter months were the road fully lit. Throughout the years, it became known as a hot-spot for couples and party goers.

Sometime during the fall of 1978, a drifter was wandering the road by himself during the early hours of the morning. Out of nowhere came a mid-size pickup truck, hitting the man and throwing him thirty feet over an embankment. After the body was discovered the next afternoon, it was determined that the drifter had been heavily drinking the night before. The driver of the truck testified that the man was wearing dark clothes and stumbled into the middle of the highway. The county prosecutor did not find any reason to charge the driver and the case was closed.

Ten years after the accident, local residents started seeing what they believed was a man wandering up and down Copperhead Ridge Road between the hours of 1am and 4am. One night a newly married couple decided they would travel up the road in their Ford F-150 for a little post wedding fun. Sometime around 2am the young couple made the long winding journey up the isolated path. They had only traveled about 200 yards when the bride began screaming in horror. This caused the groom to lock up the breaks which caused the truck to come to a complete stop. As the girl screamed, the driver tried desperately to calm her. "Honey settle down, why are you screaming...what is happening?' he said frightened. She pointed her fingers towards the front windshield. He looked but saw nothing. Unfortunately, he could not see what she was seeing. What had appeared in front of her was a ghostly figure of a man's body that was partially decomposed. The ghost was wearing a torn shirt and muddy jeans. The body kept stumbling closer and closer to the truck. As it kept getting closer, she screamed even louder. Not knowing why she was screaming, her husband reached for a flashlight and began to get out of the truck.

"Stop, please don't do that!' she screamed.

"Honey, I will show you there isn't anything out there, I promise" he said reassuringly. As he opened the driver's side door and slowly crept out of the truck, his wife suddenly stopped screaming. He turned to see why she was now quiet but she had disappeared. In sheer dread, the husband ran around to the passenger side of the truck. He flung open the door and found an empty seat where his wife once sat. He searched all around the truck, screaming her name out aloud, but never found her. So he climbed back into the truck and started driving further down the road thinking she ran away in a panic. As he kept driving, it was becoming more and more apparent that he may not see his wife ever again. As he became emotional, he started sobbing uncontrollably. All at once, his bright headlights caught a ghostly figure in the middle of the road. Upon seeing this he screamed while violently turning the steering wheel. The truck began flipping out of control and eventually landed over a steep hill.

A few hours had passed before the police and emergency responders began combing the wreckage. The crew was able to find the mangled truck but unfortunately not the bodies. After several days of exploring the road and area, the search was finally called off.

One year later, a local hunter found himself wandering down Copperhead Ridge Road in the early hours of the morning. He had been out hunting the land all day on a local ridgeline not too far away. The hunter had hiked about 200 yards down the road when his flashlight caught what he thought was the figure of a man standing in the middle of the road. As he got closer, he realized the man was more like a ghostly figure. Thinking his eyes were playing tricks on him, the hunter kept walking down the path. He finally got within about 10 yards of the figure, when he noticed the body appeared badly decomposed. This caused the hunter to scream in terror. He quickly turned around and began running the other way. In the middle of the panic, the hunter tripped over a large rock that was protruding through the mud causing him to roll down a small hill and into a briar patch. As the hunter stood up to regain his composure he heard leaves crackling and small branches snapping as if something large were walking towards him. Because he had no flashlight all the hunter could do was feel his way up the hill. As he began limping up towards the road, he heard a loud snap like someone had cracked a whip right next to his ear. He froze in terror. Even though he could not see a single thing in front or behind him, he could hear what sounded like heavy concentrated breathing. All at once a foul odor filled the woods like that of a dead animal that had been lying out in the hot sun for a week. The hunter started fast-limping up the hillside. Because the day's previous rain had washed everything out, he found himself slipping and tripping as he made his way up towards the road. As he felt his way around, he finally discovered the highway. Breathing a sigh of relief he began to walk towards what he believed was the way back off of Copperhead Ridge Road. As he slowly limped away, he heard the breathing again and smelled that awful rotten odor. Before he could take another step he heard a loud snapping noise similar to that of a tree branch being ripped apart. He turned around and screamed in horror as the face of a partially decomposed man stood in front of him.

Two years later, with multiple unsolved disappearances, the local authorities closed down Copperhead Ridge Road. To this day, nobody dares travel that desolate patch of land that creeps through the holler of that tiny West Virginia town.

Chapter 2

THE MACABRE

4

THE DEVIL IS IN
THE PUDDING

Frank Drexel was widely known to be one of the finest bakers in all of Appalachia. People came from all over just to taste Mr. Drexel's award-winning apple pies. And every October, folks would fill the street corners just to get a slice of the famous baker's pumpkin rolls. But this year was different for the old man from Crooked Creek Road in Fayette County. In early April-- to the amazement of the town--a new bakery opened up.

This particular establishment was part of a larger national bakery chain that commanded a huge customer base, wide-reaching marketing and unlimited access to grocery stores. Less than a year ago, the famous bakery had selected Fayette County for a new store due to the region's whitewater rafting and cabin-rental tourism appeal. On September 15th, *Famous Mason's Pies* had its grand opening. Not only did a clear majority of locals turn out for the spectacular event but also hundreds of tourists. The new store was literally giving away free pies and cakes to everyone in the area. It was truly a sight to see. The people lined up for blocks just to taste homemade peanut butter cookies, black walnut white chocolate cakes and the ever-most famous apple crisp pies.

It was the latter part that saddened Mr. Drexel. After decades of serving his apple pies to the local community, he was now being run out of business. For it seems corporate America had no room for a small time baker anymore.

Feeling rejected, Frank secluded himself in his house for weeks. He never left, not even to shop or attend his local church service. Nobody saw him in town, much less around his own neighborhood where he would always walk during those nice warm evenings. For days on end, he stayed locked up in his home battling severe depression. One day while fixing a sandwich, he broke down crying. As he leaned over the kitchen counter weeping loudly, he cried out, "I just want my business back. I would sell my soul to have the life I once knew given back to me."

About two months passed when Mr. Drexel received a strange knock on his front door. Unshaven and bed ridden for weeks, he had finally mustered up the strength to brew himself a fresh cup of coffee. Then, all at once, he heard two gentle taps. He paused, thinking maybe a mouse was in his cabinets. After several seconds passed, he heard three more gentle taps coming from his living room. As he made his way towards the front door, he stopped to peer out of his front window to see who it was knocking. Through the thick double paned glass he could see a very tall figure wearing all black. He didn't recognize the person but decided to open the door. "Can I help you? He asked gently.

"Frank Drexel, the Frank Drexel, right here in the flesh" the stranger said with a grin. He was a towering man; nearly seven feet tall. He wore an all-black suit with a matching fedora. His face was cleanly shaven with piercing black eyes. "Do I know you mister? Frank asked with hesitation. "No, you don't know me Frank. But I know you. And I also know you make some very delicious baked goods," the stranger said. Would you mind if I came in so we can chat? I have an offer for you." Frank gently opened the door all the way and motioned for the stranger to come inside. "You can sit if you like. I just made some coffee if you want a cup. Please excuse the clutter and my humble appearance," Frank said softly. "Sure. But I take mine black if you please, and—oh---no need to apologize for the casual dress code, my friend" the stranger said with a chilling grin.

Frank returned from his kitchen with two cups of coffee. As the stranger sipped his cup, Mr. Drexel leaned forward in his old recliner and asks. "You said you had some sort of offer for me? "Oh yes about that. I hear you are having some trouble with this new bakery that went in? In fact, I hear you don't leave your house anymore because the town has refused your deserts, the stranger said with a slight smile. "Now wait a minute, nobody said they don't like my baked food anymore!" Mr. Drexel shot back. "Look, Frank, you are getting old and your stamina just isn't there to compete with a giant like *Famous Mason's*." At this point, the stranger was practically laughing at Frank. "The people loved your food but now they have decided to move on because your recipes can't compete." the stranger said laughing. "I think it is time for you to leave!" Frank yelled. Just then the stranger

28

stood up towering over Frank. He put his coffee down and reached both hands out to Frank's. He clasped Frank's hands like a vice grip.

"Sit down Frank and listen to what I have to say."

The stranger's voice changed from friendly and soft to a dark and bellowing rhythmic bass. "Do you want to regain your footing in this town? He asked. "What do you mean, what am I going to have to do? Frank asked nervously. "Frank, I have a recipe for a pudding that the people will go crazy over. They will eat and eat and make you a very wealthy man." Frank looked puzzled. "A pudding? Frank asked with a slight quiver. "Yes Frank, a pudding. This town has never tasted a pudding quite like this. The recipe is over 1000 years old. Heck, you might even say it is biblical...hehe," the stranger laughed. "I don't understand. Why me? Frank asks. "Listen old man, I want to help you out but you have to promise me you will be here when I cash in? Promise me Frank and you will be a wealthy man that the town loves." Frank sits back down in his old recliner and reflects on what the stranger has just told him. "What do I need to do? He asks. "All you have to do is reach your hand out to me and tell me you promise that you will make the town happy, Mr. Drexel." Frank gently reaches his hand out and grasps the stranger's long fleshly hand. A sudden surge of energy rushes from Frank's fingertips searing through his torso and down to his toes. "Oh my, did you feel that mister? Frank asks trembling. "Don't worry Frank. That is just me putting the recipe into your mind. You will do well old man. You will do well," the stranger says with a large smile. Frank sits back down in his recliner and falls fast asleep.

Several hours pass when Frank finally wakes up. Startled and confused of his surroundings, he looks around the room but doesn't see the stranger. He jumps up out of his recliner and heads straight into the kitchen. In a sheer panic, he canvasses the old house, thinking it was all just a dream. He returns to his recliner and again falls asleep.

When Frank wakes up, another day had come and gone. Feeling refreshed, he goes into his kitchen to make some more coffee when he notices some unusual looking ingredients lining the countertops as if he had just come home from a busy shopping trip.

As Frank beings combing through the various grocery items, he begins to feel a sudden and familiar bolt of energy throughout his body. Without hesitation and almost as if he is on a race, the old man begins to put the ingredients to action. He moves throughout the kitchen as fast as he can. In fact, his hands are moving so fast through the mixing bowls, they are almost a blur. He runs back and forth to the pantry and refrigerator; grabbing milk, sifting sugar, pouring extract, measuring cooking oil---he is now moving at lightning speed.

An hour has passed when Frank takes a break from his feverish baking mission. He looks around the room and notices stacks upon stacks of freezable Tupper-wear containers. Excited as if it is Christmas morning and he is a small child anxiously awaiting that toy train, Frank rips the lid off of one of the containers and tastes his creation. "Oh my! Oh my!" I have done it, I am back," he begins yelling, nearly spitting out the rest of the pudding in his mouth. Frank spends the next several minutes loading container after container of pudding in his car. He then grabs a small chair and folding card table and bolts out of the door. He barrels down the highway into town, nearly ramming another vehicle as he pulls into a metered space in the middle of town square. He jumps out of his car and sets up the folding table. He then grabs his chair while he unloads nearly all of the containers of pudding he brought with him. Frank sits in his chair and patiently waits for anyone who might stop by.

Sure enough, after about five minutes had passed a young woman and her child walk up to the old baker. "Howdy ma'am," Frank says with a glee. "Would you and your son care to try some delicious homemade pudding?" "We sure would," the woman proclaims without hesitation. Frank hands them a container; grinning from ear to ear. After another few minutes had passed, another townsperson stops by Frank's table. Slowly but surely, he begins to get all of the containers handed out. After a days' worth of work, he notices he has run out of products. Frank has had one of the most successful days in a very long time.

He decides to go home for some much needed rest. When he arrives at his house, Frank goes inside, kicks off his shoes and stretches out on his couch. After dozing off, he awakens to a knock on his door. He jumps up, realizing he has slept until late in the evening. He opens the door but nobody is there. He walks back into his living room confused. He picks up a glass he had been drinking water out of earlier taking a few sips. He looks over towards his kitchen and drops the glass on the floor. Frank is startled to see the stranger standing in the doorway. "It's time Frank. It is time." the stranger says with a long face.

"T..t...t...t...time for what,? Frank says with quivering lips. The welcoming stranger now looks more sinister with a grin so evil it could turn a young man's hair snow white with one glare. "Did you just think you could cross the finish line without winning a prize Frank? Well, I allowed you to experience what you have always dreamed of. Now it's time to cash in," the stranger says with a dark smile. He takes a few steps towards Frank and reaches out his hands which are now nothing more than skeletal. He grasps Frank's shaking hands. "Be very still Mr. Drexel. Don't say a word. You're almost home my child.

Two weeks pass and nobody has heard from Frank. On this particular sunny day, a couple of teenagers riding bikes decide to stop at the old man's home. They approach the front door and begin knocking only to discover the door is ajar. One of the kids slowly pushes it open. They both walk inside cautiously. "Mr. Drexel. Mr. Drexel. Are you home?" one of the boys yells. There is no answer. "What is that smell? It smells like, like something is cooking," the older boy asks.

Both boys walk into the kitchen and see the oven light on inside. As they get closer to investigate, they see baking bowls, large spoons, an old mixer and some ingredients spread all over the countertop. "Let's get out of here. He isn't home and I don't want us to get in trouble," says the older boy. "But if he is gone, why is the oven on? Maybe he left it on accidentally. We should turn it off. It could burn the house down," the other boy proclaims. The two boys slowly walk over to the oven. Before turning it off, one of the boys pauses. He notices there is something inside. He opens the door and screams in absolute horror.

To this day Frank Drexel's home sits vacant and boarded up. The two boys never said what they saw in the oven.

5

THE MAN WITH MANY FACES

As a young child, Josh Turner was fascinated by magic. Raised by his parents in a small home outside of Grayson, Kentucky, Josh was so enamored by the art of illusion he decided to take up the talent in middle school. By the time Josh reached his senior year in high school, he was receiving invitations to travel all over the region to perform his tricks. He loved magic so much that instead of attending nearby college, Josh decided to forgo his higher education opportunities for a career as a full-time magician.

In the late fall of 1987, Josh was invited to perform at a private party at an upscale home just outside of Lexington, Kentucky. This was a great opportunity for Josh. Growing up, Josh's parents used to take him to basketball games in Lexington so he was excited to be able to return to the city where his favorite team was based. Even though the party isn't until 8pm that evening, Josh decides to leave for Lexington that morning so he has time to stop for lunch and check out the town. After getting a quick bite to eat, Josh is on his way to the mansion when he spots an antique store. He decides to stop in for a moment. Once inside, he notices the store is more like a small shop. Josh looks around in awe at the different items of antiquity. The store has a strange odor much like that of old books. After a few minutes have passed, the owner comes out from behind the counter. He is a friendly old man in his early 80s.

"Looking for anything particular?" the old man asks. "Nothing really. Just looking around. It's really neat in here. How long have you been in town?"

"Oh gosh, I arrived here in the late 40s. I was from Oklahoma originally but settled here. Hey, do you like old Native American stuff?" the old man asks.

"Well, I don't think I own anything like that but I'd love to take a look," Josh says with excitement. "Well hang on a sec, I have just the thing," the old man proclaims with enthusiasm. He walks to the back of the store and returns with a worn out leather satchel.

"That looks really cool," Josh says.

"Just wait till you see what's inside," says the old man. He opens the satchel and pulls out a piece of cloth that looks hundreds of years old. It has Native American artwork on the front with an inscription.

"What does that say?" asks Josh.

"Well, I had to give this to a friend of mine who studies Native American history over at the college. She said the words are from an old Shawnee tribe that lived in this area in the late 1700s," the old man states.

"The artwork is beautiful. But what do the words mean?" Josh asks getting anxious.

"I was told the inscription translates to Man with Many Faces," says the old man.

They both shrug and share a chuckle. Josh pays the old man for the Native American artifact and leaves.

Josh arrives at the mansion at 7:15 on the dot. It takes him approximately 20 minutes to set up everything he needs for the show. As he waits, people begin pouring in. In fact, the home owner brings in additional seating as the room nears 100 attendees. The show begins and Josh performs one trick after another. Illusion after illusion, the crowd cheers and applauds loudly. The evening is going fantastic when the home owner decides he would like everyone to take a brief 15 minute intermission to refill their drinks and get some hors d'oeuvres. As the crowd temporarily files out of the room, Josh decides to run out to his car and grab some snacks he picked up earlier. He opens the car door and retrieves his favorite peanut and chocolate candy bar. Before he closes the door, he notices something out of the corner of his eye. It is the old leather satchel he purchased earlier that day from the antique dealer. He decides to grab it as well and head back inside

Back in the home, Josh only has five minutes before the show resumes. As he quickly eats the candy, he begins studying the old Native American artifact. He reads the words out aloud. As he reads the translation, he begins speaking in Shawnee. He pauses in confusion and reads them again as if his lips and mouth are not of his control. He reads and reads in a near catatonic state. Suddenly, he is interrupted by the home owner.

"Uh, excuse me Mr. Turner, the crowd is back and ready for you to begin," the owner proclaims.

Josh sits there quiet.

"Mr. Turner, is everything alright?" he asks.

All at once Josh snaps out of his daydream.

"Yes, yes, I'm sorry. I'm not sure what just happened. I think I zoned out for a minute. I apologize," Josh says.

"Oh no worries Mr. Turner. You have been wonderful tonight. Really amazing show!" the owner says.

Josh returns to his makeshift stage in the large room of the home. He quietly looks around the audience as he begins another magic card trick. He notices a woman in her mid-30s wearing a long pink evening gown. Josh asks her to come up and pick a card out of the deck he has just shuffled. She walks up and looks at Josh, screaming in horror. Surprised, Josh stumbles backwards as she runs into the crowd.

"Ma'am, are you OK? What is wrong?" he asks shocked.

Suddenly, more members of the audience begin yelling and screaming. Josh walks out into the crowd. As he looks at each audience, they scream in horror. One woman he looks at faints. He makes his way towards a window and notices a man trying to open it.

"Sir, please!" I don't know what is happening. What is going on? Someone please tell me!" he yells. He grabs the man gently by his shoulder. As the man turns around, he screams. Josh notices in the window's reflection, his own face looks identical to the man he is looking at. He stumbles backwards into a food table knocking it over.

"Oh no, this can't be. What is happening to me?"

Josh races back into the room where he left his belongings. He quickly gathers everything and heads towards the front door. By this time, almost everyone is outside getting in their cars to leave. Still in shock, Josh fumbles to get his keys out. All at once he sees the home owner running in panic. Josh decides to run over to try one last time and calm him.

"Stay back, please stay away from me!" the owner screams at Josh. His panic causes him to run directly into a fast moving car. The owner's body is violently launched through the air. With a horrifying look, Josh runs towards the mortally wounded owner. Just as Josh is near the body, he wisps around and sees an out of control truck barreling towards him. Unsuccessfully, Josh tries to leap out of the way. The truck swerves but hits Josh. As Josh lay face down on the ground badly injured, the truck driver rushes over to him.

"Mister, are you OK? You came out of nowhere" he says emotionally distraught. The driver rolls Josh over and screams in horror. "Oh my God, this can't be. No, this can't be, this is impossible!"

The driver is staring at Josh's bloody face, only his face is now the driver's face. As the truck driver screams and begins running off, Josh slowly raises up and begins laughing hysterically.

6

THE MINFORD
MURDERS

Jesse was just a young boy when his dad began telling him a strange tale that took place in his little Appalachian hometown nestled in rural Southeastern Ohio. The story centered on a dozen rail car company salesmen who went missing back in the mid-1970s. Back then the railroad industry was the lifeblood of the local economy in Minford. A young salesman by the name of Mathias Williams was a key figure in making that industry shine. As a teenager, Mathias started as a low-level laborer, eventually working his way up to the position of sales manager. His job was to travel the region and sell rail cars and other industry equipment. He had become an expert in business-to-business sales. It was impressive for someone with little education but Mathias was turning out to be the best in his line of work.

One day while returning home from making sales calls, Mathias stopped at a gas station that doubled as a diner. He was about 25 miles outside of Minford. This particular location was one that Mathias would frequent each week during his sales routes. After he pumped gas, he went inside and ordered his usual hamburger with fries and a coke. He took a seat at one of the tables and waited for his food. The gas station diner was family run and had a small town feel to it. The owners were almost elderly but were well known and very well liked. Even though father time had caught up with them, they both worked hard in the kitchen to ensure a lifelong reputation.

Never changing his routine, Mr. Johnson, the owner, came out to greet Mathias on this day.

"Good afternoon Mathias. Glad you made it back here again," he said with a smile.

"Hey Mr. Johnson. It is great to be off that highway for a bit and I am starving," Mathias replied. "Well, we'll take good care of you as always, my friend," Mr. Johnson said.

"I know you will sir!" Mathias proclaimed.

Mr. Johnson went about greeting others. The waitress brought out Mathias' food and he began to relax and eat. While eating, he noticed a few men sitting at the diner bar area. They didn't look familiar. In fact, they looked like strangers to this town. He brushed them off as simple travelers, finished his meal and headed for the exit. He stopped at the newspaper machine, popped in a quarter and took the daily paper to read. As he walked out of the diner and back to his car, he skimmed over the front page that read, "Another Murder Strikes Our Town". After skimming through the first couple of paragraphs he gasped out aloud as he saw a picture of one of the missing persons. To his shock, he knew the face. It was Wilbur Freeman, a fellow route salesman for the company.

Mathias got in his car and kept reading. All at once, he was startled by a loud tapping on his driver's door window. It was one of those strange men from the diner. He cautiously rolled his window down. "Can I help you, sir? He asked. The stranger didn't say anything at all. "Do you need some help with something?" he asked again nervously. Once again, the stranger stood there staring at Mathias refusing to talk. Obviously frightened, Mathias rolled up his window and started his car. The radio came on so loudly it startled him. He leaned over to shut it off. When he raised back up, the stranger was gone. He paused and looked around a few times to check the area. Nobody was there. He slowly pulled out of the parking lot and onto the highway. After a mile or so of driving, his car began to act funny. The engine started seizing up on him causing the vehicle to choke along slower and slower. All at once, he noticed smoke coming out from under the hood. "Oh no, this can't be happening," Mathias said out loud. As much as he tried to pump the gas, the car kept slowing down more and more. At this point, the car was moving at about 10mph. So, Mathias made the ultimate decision to pull the car off the road.

After shutting the car off, Mathias hopped out and popped the hood to check things out. He soon realized the radiator was out of fluid. Luckily, this has happened before so he knew of a quick remedy. He walked around and opened his trunk, revealing a few jugs filled with water. He took one of the jugs and walked back to the front of his car. He poured the water into the radiator and closed the hood.

"Ahhhh!" he screamed.

As soon as he closed the hood, he saw one of the strangers from the diner standing about 10 yards behind his car. The figure wasn't doing or saying anything. He was just standing there.

Mathias sprinted to get back into his car. He looked in the rear view mirror and saw the man still standing there like a statue. He quickly turned the key but the car just kept choking and struggling to start. He turned the key over and over but nothing happened. Each time he tried to start the car, he would look in the rear view mirror. And each time he looked, the strange man appeared to be closer and closer to the car.

"Please God, start. Please start. Please start!"

One last turn and voila! The car started. He breathed a heavy sigh of relief and looked up to see if the stranger was still getting closer behind. However, the mysterious figure was no longer there. He paused for a moment to collect his thoughts and peeled away.

Mathias was about 30 minutes from his home when he realized he had forgotten to stop and pick up milk. He knew of a small grocery store a few miles ahead off Exit 91. As he approached the exit, he saw someone hitchhiking along the side of the road. As he got closer and closer, he became startled as he saw the figure.

"Oh my God, this cannot be. How is this possible?"

He slowed down as he passed the hitchhiker and sure enough, it was one of those strange men from the diner.

"This is impossible," he said scared and confused. As he passed the figure, the man lowered his thumb and just stared straight at Mathias with a blank look.

"Am I being followed? What do they want with me? This can't be a coincidence," Mathias murmured out aloud.

He was now at his exit. He quickly took the turn off of the main highway and headed straight towards his home, passing the grocery store.

"Honey, I'm sorry but I can't stop now. I will explain things when I get home," he said to himself.

The car sped down the two-lane road and around each curve. Mathias looked to his left and right, even looking in his rear view mirror. So far so good. No strange figures. He was about two streets from his home when his car started sputtering again.

"Oh no! Not now. I'm so close!" he screamed out aloud.

His car's speed was now down to a mere 10 miles per hour with a block and a half left to go. Pouring sweat and panting, Mathias focused on the last remaining leg of his trip.

He could see his house!

He pulled in his driveway, turned the car off and once again, breathed a heavy sigh of relief.

"Thank God this is all over. Now how do I explain not stopping to get the groceries," he said.

He got out of his car and made his way to the front door. He unlocked the door and saw his wife standing there.

"Sweetie!" he proclaimed loudly.

"I've never been so happy to see you baby," he said as he wrapped his arms around her.

They hugged for a minute and she shut the door.

"Mathias, honey, come with me," she spoke softly.

"Sure, but listen, I forgot to……"

"Shhhh…..its ok honey. I know you forgot to go to the store," she said calmly interrupting him.

"Come with me, there are some folks I want you to meet," she said.

"Wait, how did you know I forgot to get the groceries," he said puzzled.

As they walked into the main living room, Mathias gasped out loud.

"They are here for you, sweetie," she said with a chuckle.

"NO! NO! NO!" Mathias screamed.

All of the strange figures from the diner were standing before Mathias in his living room. They just stood there, like statues, with their outstretched arms and long creepy fingers pointing at him.

All Mathias could do was scream.

Chapter 3

Scary Places

7

McKENDREE ROAD HAUNTINGS

The residents of Hagerstown, Maryland had always known to avoid McKendree Road. The tales of strange occurrences and unexplainable events had circulated the town for years. But this time, something had unnerved the locals like never before.

It began with the couple who moved into the small, dilapidated house at the end of the road. They were young and in love, but it didn't take long for strange things to happen. They would wake up in the middle of the night to find their furniture rearranged, or their doors locked from the inside. Sometimes, they would hear whispers and footsteps that seemed to come from nowhere.

Not long after, the elderly couple in the house next door went missing, and their dog was found dead in the front yard. The police searched the area, but nothing was found. That was until a few weeks later, when the couple's bodies were found in the nearby woods, their throats slit.

The strange occurrences didn't stop there. Another resident on the road reported seeing a figure in a cloak walking through their yard, and one couple claimed that they were awakened to the sound of someone whispering in their ears. Eventually, four people were found dead and five others went missing, leaving the residents of Hagerstown to live in fear.

Rumors spread among the locals that the hauntings were caused by a cursed burial ground that lay beneath the road or perhaps the ghost of a serial killer who had once roamed the area. Others speculated that there was something inherently evil that resided on McKendree Road, waiting to torment its next victim.

The town eventually installed streetlights on the road to deter any further hauntings, but locals still avoid the area at all costs. To this day, the mystery of McKendree Road remains unsolved and is whispered about in hushed tones among those brave enough to talk about it.

8

PIKE COUNTY DISTILLERY

In the heart of Pike County, nestled deep in the woods, there stood an old moonshine distillery. It had been abandoned for years, yet the locals still talked about it as if it were the central folklore of town. They told tales of strange murmurs, shadowy figures, and eerie screams that echoed through the dark forest.

The legend went that the distillery was haunted by the ghost of a man who had been murdered there. The locals believed that he was the town drunk, a man who had spent his life swilling whiskey and causing trouble. One day, he had stumbled into the distillery, where he met a grisly fate at the hands of some ruthless bootleggers.

As the story went, the man's spirit lingered on in the distillery, filled with a burning desire for revenge. He prowled the abandoned halls, searching for his killers, driven by an insatiable thirst for blood.

Many brave souls had ventured into the distillery, eager to uncover the truth about the haunted place. But none had ever returned. The whispers of the vengeful spirit and the eerie screams kept them at bay.

Then, one stormy night, a group of teenage boys dared each other to spend the night inside the distillery. They were foolish and reckless, eager for adventure and a chance to prove themselves to their peers.

As they tiptoed through the dark halls of the distillery, they heard strange sounds and felt a cold breath upon their necks. They thought they saw shadowy figures moving in the darkness, and they heard eerie screams that seemed to come from everywhere and nowhere at once.

The boys tried to ignore these signs and pressed on, their hearts pounding with fear and excitement. As they entered a large room, they saw a figure standing in the center, wreathed in mist and bathed in an eerie blue light.

It was the ghost of the town drunk, his spectral form twisted and contorted with hatred and rage. His eyes glowed like burning coals, and he seemed to float above the ground.

The boys stood, frozen with terror, as the ghost flickered towards them, his spectral hand reaching out to drag them into the darkness.

The boys never returned from the distillery that night. And to this day, the locals are afraid to speak of the haunted moonshine distillery in Pike County. They warn travelers to stay away, lest they fall prey to the vengeful spirit that lurks within.

9

THE ALLEGHENY WITCH

Once upon a time, there was a small village nestled deep in the Allegheny Mountains of Pennsylvania. The villagers whispered of an old witch who lived in a cabin on the outskirts of town. According to legend, the witch had lived in the area for over a hundred years and anyone who dared to seek her out would suffer her wicked curse.

Many brave souls tried to uncover the truth about the witch, but none returned to share their findings. They disappeared without a trace, leaving their loved ones to wonder what had become of them. As the years went by, the stories of the witch's evil grew stronger, and the villagers became even more afraid of her.

One day, a young man named John decided to put an end to the rumors and uncover the truth about the witch. He set out for the cabin, determined to discover the truth and prove that the witch was nothing more than a myth.

As John approached the cabin, he felt a sense of dread wash over him. The wind howled, and the trees rustled, warning him to stay away. But John was not afraid. He approached the door and knocked.

For a moment, there was no answer, and John thought he had been foolish to come. But then the door creaked open, and a hunched old woman appeared. Her eyes were cloudy, and her skin was wrinkled, and she looked much older than the hundred years the villagers had claimed.

"Who are you?" she croaked, her voice creaking like an old door.

"My name is John, and I've come to prove that you're not the witch everyone says you are," he said.

The old woman laughed, a cruel sound that seemed to echo in the stillness of the woods. "Is that so?" she said. "Well, I'm afraid you're too late. The curse has already taken hold."

John looked around, but there was nothing out of the ordinary. "What curse?" he asked.

"The curse of the witch," she said, her eyes gleaming with malice. "Anyone who comes seeking me will be cursed themselves. You will disappear, just like all the others."

John thought he saw a flicker of something in the old woman's eyes, a hint of remorse, maybe. But then it was gone, replaced by the same sinister glint that had been there before.

As he turned to leave, the old woman beckoned him back. "Wait," she said. "Take this. "She handed him a small charm, a twisted piece of metal that looked like it had been shaped by some dark magic. "It will protect you," she said. "But you must leave this place at once, before the curse takes hold."

John didn't know what to think, but he took the charm and fled. He didn't stop running until he was safely back in the village, where he discovered that the charm did indeed seem to protect him from harm.

But despite his success in escaping the witch's grasp, John could never shake the feeling that there was something still lurking in the woods, watching him, waiting to claim him as its next victim. And as long as the old witch remained in her cabin, the legend would continue to haunt the Allegheny Mountains, claiming the lives of anyone foolish enough to venture too close.

Chapter 4

HAUNTINGS

10

THE HAUNTED ORGAN

Justin and Sarah had just moved into their new house and were eager to decorate it with antiques. On a sunny Saturday morning, they visited a local flea market and stumbled upon an early 1800s antique organ. It was intricate, with carved patterns and dark wooden keys. The couple were mesmerized by its beauty and decided to purchase it. As the couple carried the organ into their home, they noticed a strange feeling in the air. It was as if someone was watching them. However, they brushed it off as nerves and continued to install the organ in their living room.

As the sun began to set, Justin sat at the organ and began to play a few notes. It sounded beautiful, the notes echoing through the room. Sarah sat back and listened to her boyfriend's playing, but as he went on, she noticed something strange. The room began to darken, and everything seemed to move in slow motion.

Justin stopped playing, noticing the strange occurrences. Suddenly, the room went silent. They both got up and walked around, inspecting the area. Then, out of nowhere, the organ began to play itself. Its keys moving independently as if something was controlling it.

The couple were terrified, frozen in place. Then, a voice spoke to them from the organ, and they could feel an ominous presence. They knew the organ was haunted. The couple attempted to flee the house, but the doors were locked, trapping them inside.

The organ continued to play, and the couple began to feel like they were losing their minds. Then, without warning, one of them was violently attacked. The other tried to intervene, but it was too late. The evil presence had taken control, and they were both trapped, unable to escape their haunted home.

The next day, the police were called to the scene after their neighbors couldn't get an answer on either of the couple's cell phones. They found the couple dead, their bodies mutilated. The antique organ, once a beautiful piece of history, was left untouched, reminding all who entered the house of the sinister presence that still haunted the home.

11

THEY WILL FIND YOU

Frank entered the antique store, and he couldn't help but feel a sense of nostalgia wash over him. As he walked past the old picture frames and antique furniture, he felt a sense of peace. But he knew he had to remain focused for his daughter's sake. He had promised to find her something special for her birthday, and she had always been fascinated with Native American folklore. He hoped that he could find something that would make her happy.

His eyes locked onto a small leather-bound book, tucked away in the corner. It looked ancient and almost out of place among the other things on display. Curiosity got the better of him, and he walked over to take a closer look. The book was titled "Burial Chants of the Iroquois."

Frank picked up the book and examined it. It was old, and the pages were yellowed with age. The cover was rough and worn, and the spine creaked when he opened it. The pages were filled with old Native American chants and incantations. He couldn't help but feel the weight of the book in his hands. It was as if the book was calling out to him.

He knew he had to buy it.

Frank purchased the book and headed home. He couldn't wait to see his daughter's face when she received her gift. However, he had no idea what was in store for them.

After a few days, Frank's daughter, Bailey, finally had some free time to settle down with her new book. She decided to recite one of the chants aloud, curious to see if anything would happen.

To her surprise, the moment she finished chanting, an eerie silence fell over the house. It was as if time had stopped. Suddenly, a gust of wind rattled the windows, and the room began to shake like a tremor had struck the house.

The air grew colder, and Bailey felt a sense of fear creeping up her spine. She remembered her father telling her that the chants were ancient, and they should not be trifled with. But it was too late. The spirits had been released.

Out of the shadows, a horde of evil spirits emerged. They were all around her, and she could sense their malevolent intent. They were angry, vengeful spirits that wanted nothing more than to cause chaos and destruction.

Bailey screamed, and Frank rushed in, trying to shield her from the spirits. But it was no use. They surrounded them, and the more they tried to run, the closer the spirits got. They couldn't escape.

Frank and Bailey had no choice but to run. The father and daughter duo decided to grab a few suitcases full of their clothes and some belongings and ran to the car.

They fled from their home, their town, and their state. They traveled for days, never stopping for anything, but the spirits were relentless. No matter where they went, the spirits found them.

As they journeyed through different towns, Bailey noticed that her father was becoming increasingly paranoid. He kept mumbling under his breath, as if he feared that someone was watching them. She didn't understand what was happening, but she knew it had something to do with the book.

The spirits were still with them, and they could feel their presence growing stronger. The wind would pick up, and the temperature would drop when the entities were near. Frank was desperate to find a solution, but he knew that he was up against something far beyond his understanding.

Fresh out of places to run, Frank and Bailey finally found a state park to sleep overnight. As the spirits circled their car, the duo knew they would have to confront them once and for all. They both got out of the car and stood face-to-face with the spirits.

After a brief moment of staring, the spirits led them deep into the woods, where an old Native American burial ground lay. Then, the entities chanted in unison, and the earth began to tremble. The ground split open, and a dark hole appeared in front of them.

The spirits grabbed hold of Frank and Bailey, dragging them into the hole. They fell into the abyss, and the darkness swallowed them whole. The only sound that could be heard was the distant chanting of the spirits as they continued their evil work.

The spirits had won. They were here to stay, following whomever dared.

12

SPOONS IN THE GRAVEYARD

Regina was old and wrinkled, her eyes a piercing blue that seemed to hold secrets untold. She lived in a small, rundown house on the outskirts of town, and not many people knew her or what she did.

But there were rumors that she collected strange things – bones, mostly. Some speculated that the reason for her strange habit was because she was a witch, while others believed that she was just an odd old lady with a penchant for the macabre.

Either way, nobody dared to venture too close to her home. They say that strange things happen around her, and anyone who dared bother her would end up being part of her collection.

One night, however, a group of high school seniors dared one another to sneak into her yard and find out the truth about what Regina was really up to. They crept through the shadows, making their way through the overgrown weeds and bushes. And when they finally arrived at her doorstep, they couldn't believe what they saw.

Bones – hundreds of them – lined the walls of her little house. They were stacked up to the ceiling, arranged in neat rows like a morbid museum exhibit. And in the center of it all was Regina, hovering over a boiling cauldron filled with something that looked like soup.

"What are you doing?" asked one of the teens, his voice trembling.

"I'm making soup," Regina replied in a matter-of-fact tone. "Would you like to try some?"

"What's in it?" asked another, his voice shaking with fear.

Regina smiled, a grin that made the hairs on their necks stand up. "It's an old family recipe," she said, stirring the cauldron with a long wooden spoon. "It's made with very special ingredients."

The teens took a step back, suddenly feeling very afraid. And then, they heard a sound that chilled them to the bone – footsteps, coming from all around them.

Regina chuckled. "It looks like my little secret is out," she said, turning to face them. "But don't worry – now that you're here, you can help me."

And with that, she dipped her spoon into the cauldron and sloshed it onto the floor. Something emerged from the depths of the soup, something that was half-human, half-skeleton.

The teenagers screamed, but it was too late – they were already surrounded by the undead. Regina cackled with glee, knowing that her plan to bring back all the dead in town to do her bidding had finally come to fruition.

Panicked, one of the teens tried to make a run for it but was stopped dead in his tracks by one of Regina's zombies.

The undead figured grabbed the teen and bit his neck, leaving a bloody gash. The teen just fell to the ground. The zombie then picked up the lifeless body and dumped it head first into the boiling vat of putrid soup.

This caused the other teens to run in chaos. But one by one the zombies attacked the teens and put each in the soup pot until they were all gone.

And as for the soup?

It was said that those who tasted it never lived to tell the tale – they became part of Regina's ever-growing collection of bones, a grim reminder of her twisted recipe for immortality.

Chapter 5

COAL CAMP LEGENDS

13

KING SOLOMON'S REVENGE

Solomon had always known that being a coal miner was a dangerous job. However, he never thought he would meet his end in such a cruel way. It was the mid-1900s, and Davidson, Tennessee, was a small town where racism ran rampant. Solomon was one of the few black miners in the coal mine and always felt like an outcast.

However, he did his job quietly, never speaking up or complaining. He was a proficient worker who loved to whistle church hymns while he labored. While he knew he was not liked very well, he kept his head down and did as he was told.

That was until the day he overheard a group of white miners plotting against him.

They planned to create a fake accident that would leave Solomon trapped in the mine, and they wouldn't rescue him. The miner's thought their plan was foolproof, but Solomon's instincts told him that something was off.

So, when the fake accident happened, Solomon tried to escape. But the group of white miners was waiting for him at the mine's entrance. They had closed the entrance with dynamite, trapping Solomon inside.

With no way out, and air quality becoming increasingly bad, Solomon resigned himself to his fate. He was going to die in that mine, and nobody would ever know what happened to him.

Days turned into weeks, and weeks turned into months. Solomon's body never left the mine. He was left to rot among the coal for years.

But then something strange happened. Miners started to disappear. They would simply vanish without a trace, leaving behind no clues as to what had happened to them. The remaining miner's began to whisper about Solomon's ghost seeking revenge on the group of white miners who left him to die. The whispers turned into screams when one of the white miners was found dead in his house. A few days later, another miner was found dead in the middle of the woods from hypothermia. A week after that, a third miner was deceased, found face down in a shallow creek. The death was ruled an accidental drowning but many questioned the coroner's report since the water was only a couple of feet deep.

The other miners knew it was the work of Solomon's vengeful spirit. The remaining miners fled the town, never to return again.

But Solomon's ghost still lingers in the coal mine, waiting for more miners to exact his revenge on. Even to this day, the mine remains abandoned, too dangerous for anyone to enter. Some say you can still hear Solomon's whistling echoing through the mine's empty tunnels, warning all those who dare to enter about the consequences of their actions.

14

THE BETSY LANE DISASTER

The small mining town of Betsy Lane, Kentucky had always been a quiet and peaceful place. It was the perfect backdrop for Americana. Each year the townsfolk would gather for annual parades, festivals and their biggest event; the town Christmas tree lighting ceremony. Crime was so low that most folks went to sleep with windows open and doors unlocked. Everyone knew each other and got along like family. And the mine had been the central economic hub for the town for nearly a hundred years. The mine owner was an old likeable fella who treated his miners with respect and tried to give out a pay-raise annually. As a result, the town kept growing each year, slowly adding new businesses.

Unfortunately, everything changed when the disaster happened.

It was just another typical autumn day at the mine when something went terribly wrong. No one knew exactly what happened, but suddenly a massive explosion shook the entire mine. After the dust settled, it became clear that the miners were trapped inside, and there was no way to get them out.

The families of the miners waited outside for hours, hoping for some sign of hope, but it wasn't until the early morning hours of the following day they finally heard something. Screams and moans erupted from the mine entrance as some of the miners stumbled out. They were pale, covered in dirt and blood, and their eyes were vacant.

A strange smell covered the air like a toxic blanket.

The survivors were taken to the hospital, where they were tested for any signs of sickness or infection. Nothing seemed out of the ordinary, until one of the miners suddenly began vomited a black like tar substance. He leaped off of the hospital bed and began screaming and clawing at his own flesh. A nurse rushed in to see if she could help the man but he attacked and bit her arm. His teeth tore a six inch chunk out of her forearm, spraying blood all over the bed and floor. The nurse grabbed her arm and fell backwards and slammed her head into a piece of medical equipment causing an annoying bell to go off.

Three other nurses came sprinting into the room but before anyone could react, the injured nurse began to transform into something else entirely. Her eyes became completely bloodshot and she began vomiting the same black tar-like substance the coal miner had. She screamed in horror and began biting at anything and everything.

Terrified, the staff tried to keep the nurse under control, but it was too late. The miner grabbed another staffer and bit him. The entire room was in chaos. The hospital's only security guard, who was on another floor, came rushing into the room to find the entire staff had transformed. He slammed the door shut; holding the door as hard as he could. He began yelling for everyone to run but his hands gave out and he fell to the ground.

The infected staff rushed the weak guard, tearing at his flesh. Afterwards, they made their way around the second floor of the hospital, biting and infecting others. Eventually, the entire hospital was under siege.

As the day turned into night, the virus spread throughout the town, turning people into flesh eating zombies that attacked and killed each other.

The once peaceful streets of Betsy Lane were now overrun with the undead. The Kentucky State Police and National Guard were called in to quarantine the town, but it was already too late.

The virus had already made its way into the rest of the county, and soon enough, it was spreading throughout the entire state.

The mining disaster that happened in Betsy Lane was a tragedy that would never be forgotten. It not only claimed the lives of hundreds of miners, but it resulted in the release of a chemical that turned the entire town into a living nightmare. And now, the world would forever be changed, all because of one terrible accident in a small town in Kentucky.

15

THE GRUNDY KILLER

The small town of Grundy, Virginia had always been a quaint place, nestled in the heart of the Appalachian Mountains. But that all changed when William Folks came to town. The townspeople were huddled inside their homes, locked doors and windows in fear of the notorious serial killer, William Folks. Folks was a former coal miner who had turned to a life of murder and mayhem, leaving a trail of mutilated bodies in his wake.

Legend has it he was drunk one night and decided to play with an Ouija board and a set of Tarot cards. A short while later he became demon possessed.

The people of Grundy had always known there was something off about Folks. He had a wild, unpredictable look in his eyes and a tendency to lash out at anyone who crossed him. But no one suspected him of murder until the first body turned up. It was a young woman, barely out of high school, who had been found in a ditch on the outskirts of town. Her body had been sliced open from neck to groin, her organs spilling out onto the ground. It was a scene straight out of a horror movie, and the people of Grundy were mortified.

But the terror was just beginning.

In the weeks that followed, more bodies turned up. Each one more gruesome than the last. Folks seemed to be growing bolder, killing in broad daylight and leaving his victims out in the open for all to see.

The police were at a loss.

They had no leads, no suspects, and no idea how to stop this madman from terrorizing their town. The people of Grundy began to feel like prisoners in their own homes, afraid to venture out after dark.

And then, one night, Folks struck again.

This time, he targeted a family of five, breaking into their home and slaughtering them in their beds. The scene was so horrific that even the seasoned police officers who responded to the call were shaken, with many vomiting from the sight. It was then that they realized Folks wasn't just a serial killer. He was a monster, a force of evil that couldn't be stopped by normal means.

The people of Grundy knew they had to take matters into their own hands.

They formed vigilante groups, patrolling the streets at night with guns and knives, ready to take down Folks if they crossed paths with him. It was a dangerous game, but they felt they had no choice.

And then, one night, their worst fears were realized.

Folks appeared on the street, his eyes wild with rage and his hands stained with blood. The vigilantes didn't hesitate. They opened fire, their bullets tearing into Folk's flesh. But as the smoke cleared and the body was examined, the people of Grundy realized with horror that they had made a mistake.

The man they had killed wasn't Folks at all. It was just an innocent homeless drunk who had been in the wrong place at the wrong time.

And Folks?

He was still out there, somewhere, watching and waiting for his next victim. The people of Grundy knew they could never let their guard down again.

They were living in a horror story, and there was no end in sight.

Chapter 6

SUPERNATURAL FORCES

16
WHITEWATER EVIL

Tina and Rachel had been planning their summer adventure for months. They were both college students from Colorado who loved the thrill of adventure. When they heard about the whitewater rapids in Fayetteville, West Virginia, they knew that was the perfect destination. They packed their bags, loaded up the car, and set off on their journey.

As they drove through the winding roads of the mountains, they couldn't help but feel excited about what was to come. The scenery was beautiful, the air was fresh, and the anticipation of the whitewater rapids made their hearts race.

When they finally arrived at the campsite, they were welcomed by the rushing sound of the river. They set up their tent and decided to go for a quick dip in the river before the sun went down. However, as they entered the water, they noticed something strange.

The water was freezing cold, even though it was the middle of summer. It also had an odd green tint that seemed to be in a portion of the river. They shrugged it off and decided to have fun anyway, but things took a dark turn quickly.

A few seconds after getting in, the water began to swirl around them, pulling them under and tossing them around like rag dolls. They struggled to break free from the current, but it was too strong.

As they surfaced, they heard screams coming from downstream. They swam towards the noise and saw a group of tourists struggling to stay afloat a raft. Tina and Rachel quickly swam over and tried to help, but they couldn't hold on for long. The tourists were dragged under, one by one, and disappeared without a trace.

Tina and Rachel knew they had to get out of the water immediately, but as they tried to make their way back to shore, they realized they were surrounded by an invisible force. The water kept pulling them under and back and forth. It was almost as if it was playing with them.

The girls also quickly realized the water had become a deadly supernatural force that was killing tourists up and down the river.

After struggling for a few minutes, Tina was able to grab a hold of a protruding rock structure and lift herself out of the water. She then grabbed Rachel by the leg and drug her up out of the evil current. Barely able to catch their breath, bruised and in a semi-state of shock, the girls managed to pull it together and run back to their campsite. To their surprise, the water had invaded their tent, and their belongings were floating in the river. They knew they had to leave before it was too late, but the force was too strong, and they were trapped. The water was now everywhere. They could see numerous dead bodies of tourists floating about.

Luckily the girls found a large rock bank that they climbed. They laid down in relief, if only temporary.

As the night fell, they huddled together in fear, listening to the screams of the remaining tourists being pulled under by the water. They knew they were next. The water continued to rise, and they could feel its cold embrace around their ankles.

Suddenly, a figure appeared out of nowhere. It was an old man who looked like he had been living in the mountains for decades. He told them the legend of the river and how it was cursed by the spirits of the natives who had been killed by the settlers.

He gave them a map to the only safe route out of the mountains and warned them not to look back. Tina and Rachel took the map, climbed off of the rock bed and ran for their lives. They followed the path, not daring to turn around, and finally made it out of the mountains.

They looked back and saw the river glowing in the darkness, and they knew that they had narrowly escaped a deadly fate.

From that day on, they never spoke of the cursed river again and avoided any mention of whitewater country in West Virginia. The memory of that night haunted them for the rest of their lives.

17

THE WINDS OF WHITLEY

It was a warm summer evening in Whitley County, Kentucky, and the sun had just set behind the rolling hills that surrounded the small rural community. The air was still and quiet, save for the occasional chirp of crickets and the rustling of leaves in the gentle breeze.

But then, something changed.

A giant gust of wind began to sweep through the county, blowing over trees and knocking down power lines. It was so strong that people could feel their homes shaking and the ground beneath their feet trembling.

The residents were in total shock. Their worst nightmare had come true; a tornado was destroying the area.

Or was it?

Suddenly, the wind started to subside as quickly as it started. The people slowly came back out of their homes and got out of their cars, looking around in disbelief. That's when all hell began to break loose.

One by one, a piercing burning sensation began spreading throughout each person's eyes and throats. At first, everyone thought it was a weird reaction to the wind gust and tried to ignore it. But soon, they began to feel dizzy and disoriented, as if they were all under the influence of some powerful drug. Their thoughts became muddled, and their vision blurred. They began stumbling around like drunkards, struggling to maintain their balance.

As the night progressed, things got worse.

The people of Whitley began to feel a strange hunger, a gnawing hunger that could not be satisfied by food. Their mouths watered, and their eyes turned yellow as if jaundiced. They became restless, pacing back and forth muttering to themselves incoherently.

Then, the unthinkable happened.

A man attacked his neighbor, biting off a chunk of his flesh with his teeth. The victim screamed in agony, and the attacker continued to devour him, ignoring his pleas for mercy. Soon, others joined in, and the county descended into chaos.

The sheriff's office was inundated with calls reporting violent attacks all over the county. But when the deputies arrived, they found the streets filled with crazed, cannibalistic residents who had lost all sense of humanity. It was as if some unseen force had possessed them, turning them into mindless rabid monsters.

The authorities tried to contain the outbreak, but it was too late.

The infected were multiplying, and the death toll was rising quickly. The county was plunged into darkness as the power grid failed, and the survivors were left to fend for themselves in a world of madness and horror.

The weeks that followed were a nightmare. The infected roamed the streets, hunting for fresh prey. The survivors huddled in their homes, trying to fortify their defenses and protect themselves from the relentless onslaught. But it was a losing battle. The infected were too numerous, too ferocious, and too hungry to be stopped.

In the end, only a handful of people survived the apocalypse that had engulfed Whitley County.

They fled the area, leaving the ruins of their homes and the memories of the unspeakable horrors they had witnessed. No one knew where the wind had come from, or what supernatural force had unleashed the chemical that turned the locals into cannibals.

But one thing was certain; they would never forget the day the wind blew in, bringing with it, the end of their community as they knew it.

18

FIRE ON THE MOUNTAIN

In the heart of the Appalachian Mountains, deep in the woods, there lived an old mountain family. They were a mysterious clan, known for their strange powers that came from drinking a special type of moonshine. It was said that the family could control fire, and many in the surrounding towns believed them to be witches and warlocks.

The family had lived in the mountains for generations, and they had always kept to themselves. They lived in a small cabin made of logs, surrounded by trees and mountains. The family had a reputation for being unfriendly, and they rarely spoke to anyone outside of their clan.

One day, a group of escaped prison inmates stumbled across the mountain family while on the run from the cops.

The inmates were dangerous, psychotic men who had killed several guards during their escape. They were desperate for food and shelter, and they saw the mountain family as an easy target. The inmates approached the family's cabin and demanded what

ASHLEY C. STINNETT

they desired. The family knew they were in danger, but they also knew they had a special power that could protect them. They invited the inmates inside and offered them some moonshine.

The inmates eagerly accepted the offer, not realizing that the moonshine was the source of the family's power. As the convicts drank the white lightning, the family began to chant and perform a ritual. Confused, the inmates looked around in anger.

"Stop that," one of them yelled.

The family kept chanting. The inmates grew irate.

"Stop that noise and give us what we want. As a matter of fact, we're just gonna take it all from ya," the inmate said.

The inmate reached out to choke one of the family members but he couldn't move his feet.

"What is happening here," he asked.

Suddenly, the room burst into flames, and the inmates were trapped. The family used their power to control and direct the fire towards the convicts. The group tried to escape, but the flames surrounded them and were too high. They screamed and begged for the family to stop, but the mountain clan ignored their pleas.

They continued to control the fire until every inmate was burned to death.

The family emerged from their cabin unscathed, and they knew that they had been successful in defending themselves. They had used their power to protect themselves from the dangerous inmates and they had succeeded.

Word of the incident quickly spread, and many in the surrounding towns and communities were frightened by the family's power. Some even believed that the family was cursed and should be avoided at all costs.

But the family didn't care about what others thought.

Chapter 7

DEADLY DWELLINGS

19

THE LEGEND OF PUMPKIN TOOTH HOUSE

Once upon a time, in the small town of Greenville, South Carolina, there lived an old reclusive man in a house near the end of Autumn Street. The man was known to the locals as a creepy old guy who had a strange obsession with pumpkins. Every year, as Halloween approached, he would decorate his entire house with pumpkins.

But these were not just any ordinary pumpkins; they looked creepy, and the jack-o-lanterns always had these weird looking teeth inside of them.

The local townspeople were always afraid of him, and they warned their children to stay away from his house, especially during Halloween. But despite their warnings, there were always a few curious souls who would venture near his property to take a look at the spooky decorations.

One year, a group of high school teenagers decided to see what those pumpkins were really made of. They were intrigued by the creepy decorations and wanted to see the secret behind the old man's obsession with pumpkins.

One evening, right before Halloween, the teenagers trespassed onto his property. They sneaked in through the back gate and made their way towards the house. As they approached the front porch, they noticed that the jack-o-lanterns were even more grotesque than they had imagined. The pumpkins had strange markings and carvings on them, and the teeth inside looked like they belonged to something other than a pumpkin.

Suddenly, one of the teens heard a noise coming from the inside the house. They froze in fear, and as they turned around, they saw the old man staring at them from the window. His eyes were cold and lifeless, and his face was twisted into a grotesque smile.

The teenagers tried to run, but the old man had already stepped out of the house and was blocking their path.

He was holding a large knife in his hand, and his eyes were fixed on the teenagers. As they stood frozen in fear, the old man started to speak. He told them that he had been stealing dead bodies from the local cemetery for years. He would take the teeth from the corpses and use them to create the grotesque teeth inside the jack-o-lanterns.

The teenagers were horrified at what they heard.

They tried to run again, but the old man was too fast for them. He caught up with them and one, by one, dragged them back into the house.

Once inside, the old man locked the doors and started to prepare his tools. The teens were screaming and begging for him to let them go, but the old man did not listen. He was determined to make them pay for trespassing onto his property.

The old man slowly paced around the decrepit house that wreaked like burnt hair and onions.

The floors were scummy; covered with the rotten remnants of pumpkins and newspapers. He just walked around mindlessly, looking up at the ceiling and down at the floor. One of the teens screamed and it seemed to snap him out of whatever trance he was in.

He grabbed an old drill that was plugged into an extension cord. He ran after the teen with the drill.

As the night wore on, the screams of the teenagers grew fainter and fainter until they were silenced altogether. The old man had gotten rid of the evidence, and there was no trace of the teenagers left behind.

The next day, the townspeople noticed that the old man's house was quiet. There was no more spooky decorations, and the old man had disappeared without a trace. But the memory of what had happened would haunt the town for years to come.

From that day on, the locals would never forget the old man who lived at the end of Autumn Street. His legacy would live on through the legends and rumors that circulated around the town. And every Halloween, the townspeople would remember the horrors that had taken place in the old man's house, and they would shudder with fear at the thought of what might have happened if they had been the ones to trespass onto his property.

20

THE STRANGE PICTURE ON THE WALL

One year, a young family from Atlanta, longing for a quiet life, decided to move from the hustle and bustle of the city. They decided to move to an old farmhouse in Habersham County, Georgia near Tallulah Falls. The sprawling countryside and peacefulness of the Appalachian region drew them to the property and they couldn't wait to start their new life there.

As they were unpacking their belongings, they noticed a large family portrait hanging on the wall in the dining room. It was a beautiful painting, depicting a family of six, all smiling and happy. The father, mother, and four children all looked like they had been frozen in time, captured in the prime of their lives.

The family didn't think nothing of it at first, but a few nights after settling in, they noticed something strange. The portrait had started bleeding. A trickle of blood was oozing from the father's mouth and trickling down his chin. The mother's eyes seem to follow them around the room, and the children's faces seemed to be contorted in pain.

The family was understandably horrified, but they couldn't explain what was happening. They tried to ignore it, thinking it was just their imagination playing tricks on them. But every night the portrait continued to bleed, the blood staining the wall and dripping onto the floor.

As time passed, the family began to notice other strange occurrences. Doors would open and close by themselves, and they would hear strange noises coming from the walls. One day, they found a small hole in the dining room wall, and when they looked inside, they found a horrifying secret. The family that had lived in the home before them was behind the wall. Their bodies were decomposing, and the smell was unbearable. It was clear that they had been murdered, but by whom and why was a mystery. The previous family had vanished without a trace, and no one in the area had heard from them in years.

The young family from Atlanta realized they had moved into a house with a dark and twisted past. The portrait bleeding was just the beginning of the horror that awaited them. They knew they had to leave, but the evil in the house wasn't going to let them go so easily.

Every night, they were tormented by the spirts of the previous family and they knew they had to find a way to put them to rest before it was too late.

In the end, the family never got their peaceful country life. They moved out of the farmhouse as quickly as they could, haunted by memories of what they had seen and experienced. The portrait that had once hung on the dining room wall was left behind, a reminder of the terror they had faced.

21

A Funhouse to Die For

O nce a year, the carnival would arrive in Pomeroy, Ohio. The townsfolk would eagerly await its arrival, looking forward to the rides and the games that would be set up in the town square. But in recent years, something had changed. The carnival had become darker, more sinister. And the people of the town had begun to fear it.

The carnival arrived one day during the early morning hours, rolling into town on a convoy of battered old trucks and trailers. The carnies were a strange bunch, their faces twisted and scarred, their eyes glittering with madness. They set up their tents and rides in the town square, and the people of Pomeroy watched with a mix of curiosity and unease.

At first, everything seemed normal. The carnival rides were popular with the locals, and the children squealed with delight as they spun around and around on the Ferris wheel. But things took a dark turn rather quickly.

It started with rumors of disappearances. A child here, a teenager there, vanishing without a trace. At first, no one believed it. But as more and more people went missing, the residents started to panic. And then came the screams. Late at night, when the carnival was closed, the locals would hear the terrified screams of its victims. They tried to investigate, but the carnival was always locked up tight, with nobody around to hear their pleas for help.

The carnival's funhouse was the center of the rumors. It was a ramshackle old building, with peeling paint and creaking floorboards. It was said that anyone who dared to enter would never return.

One night, a group of college students who were home for the summer, decided to investigate. They crept up to the funhouse under cover of darkness, determined to uncover the truth. But they never came back. Their bodies were found the next day, mangled and twisted beyond recognition.

It wasn't long before the townsfolk began to suspect that something truly evil was going on inside the carnival. They started to steer clear of it, telling their children to stay away. But the carnival seemed to have a life of its own, growing in power with each passing year.

One night, a group of brave locals decided to take matters into their own hands. Armed with flashlights and weapons, they stormed the carnival grounds, determined to put a stop to the terror once and for all.

But what they found was beyond anything they could have imagined.

The carnival was alive, a monstrous entity that fed on the fear and terror of its victims. It had been using the town of Pomeroy as its own personal feeding grounds, luring people in with the promise of fun and excitement, only to slaughter them in the dead of night.

Chapter 8

Mountain Creatures

22

THE RUSTY SHACKLES

Deep in the heart of Wyoming County, West Virginia is a public meeting place called the Rusty Shackles. Some would refer to it as a dive bar while others simply know it as a county landmark. Whatever one chooses to call it-- there is no question--this place has been the center of legends for nearly 60 years.

One late summer weekend, a group of friends from New York were traveling the hills of West Virginia as part of a week-long Appalachian tour. They decided to stop in the southern part of the state to check out mountain hiking and whitewater rafting.

A short time after arriving in the Pineville area, they discovered their next destination.

"Hey, there is this place called The Rusty Shackles. It looks like everybody around here has something to say about it on social media. Unfortunately there aren't very many reviews, but it sounds sick," exclaimed one of the friends.

"Heck Yeah! Why don't we hit it up and see? It looks like it's only a few miles away," the other friend said with excitement.

After a few moments of deliberation, the group of four set out to find the bar.

Not being able to rely on a GPS due to choppy cell service, the group had to trust finding the establishment the old fashioned way.

After walking a couple of miles, the foursome spotted an old country gas station that was still in operation.

The friends went inside.

All around, the room smelled of burnt coffee, bad cologne and cigarettes.

"Excuse me. Do you, by chance, know where there is a place called The Rusty Shackles?' one of the friends asked.

The old man behind the cash register sat there with a cup of coffee and a newspaper. He didn't make a motion as if not to hear the question.

One of the friends grabbed a travel mug that had the words, "Almost Heaven" inscribed on the side. He took it over to the old-fashioned style coffee maker that was on the checkout counter.

"How long has this coffee been brewing?" he asked.

The old man perked up a little bit.

"About a half hour. I brewed it myself," he proclaimed.

"Man, I love coffee. Have you had that brand Southern Coal Fire?" the friend asked.

Now the old man's attention was completely on the group.

"Oh, absolutely. We sell that a lot. Folks love it a bunch around here, "the old man said with excitement.

"Hey, where did you say you were trying to get to? He asked.

"The Rusty Shackles," one of the friends said.

The old man slowly put down his coffee, folded the newspaper in half and tossed it aside. He gently rose up out of his chair and began looking at each and every one of the group members.

"Ya'll stay away from that place. You hear me. It aint no good. It aint never been no good. I can tell ya'll are traveling. Those accents are up north. Don't go in there. A lot of crazy and stupid people are in there, doin bad things," he said sternly.

One of the friends spoke up.

"Mister, we can handle it. You are right, we are from up north. The big city to be exact. New York. So, obviously we have been in plenty of bad places and survived. We are down here checking out your beautiful state. Look, two of us played football so we can handle ourselves. I even got a letter from Marshall about it," he said with glee.

The old man studied over the two men.

"You fellas look tough. But I'm telling ya, it aint a good place. But if you're achin to get a fix, then you're only a mile away. Keep down the main road, then turn at the left fork of Adkins Branch. You can't miss the building. Only one out there. Good luck to ya," he said.

The old man sat down, opened up his newspaper and began sipping his coffee.

"Thanks man!

The friends left the gas station and headed down the highway. By this time, it was around 8pm.

After walking exactly one mile, they spotted the bar.

"There it is," one of the friends shouted.

There it stood, like a giant piece of history. The building was very old on the outside. It had worn out black and brown paint. The structure looked like it was from a bygone coal camp era. The sign read, "The Rusty Shackles" with an old pair of chains hanging from the end of the words.

"Oh my God, this is amazing!" shouted one of the friends.

"Let's get this party started folks!" the other one yelled.

The four friends went inside.

As they entered, the inside was filled with a thick fog of cigarette smoke. An antique looking brightly lit juke box blasted an old George Jones song. There were three or four older men playing pool towards the side of the room. Seated at the bar were about a half a dozen men ranging in age.

"Wow, this is definitely the entertainment spot bro. Not one single person our age," he said chuckling.

"Let's just grab a beer and make this quick," the other friend said disappointed.

The four walked up to the bar and took a seat.

The bartender, who was busy washing dishes, didn't notice the four.

"Excuse me bartender, we would like to get some drinks,"

The bartender turned around and the four friends gasped. He was an old man, probably in his early 70s. He had a huge scar that started above his left eye and snaked down the side of his face and onto his upper neck. His hair was greasy looking and in a ponytail. His forearms were covered in old military tattoos, with one being a large navy anchor. He approached them slowly.

"You boys and that accent," he said with a deep raspy baritone voice.

The friends just sat there looking at him in amazement.

"Well don't be scared of me fellas. Welcome to The Rusty Shackles," he said with a laugh.

The four friends laughed along.

About two hours had passed. The friends drank beer and listened to the bartenders stories that varied from military service, marriage and being in prison for robbery.

"Man this beer is hitting me hard. I've only had a few," one of the friends said with slurred speech.

"It's Appalachian beer dude," the other said with a buzz.

"He aint lying. This is some of the best craft beer around here. It's gotta little bit of white lightning bred in it," the bartender said proudly.

The four continued to slam beers and laugh at stories. Another hour had passed.

"Holy crap, it's pushing midnight and we gotta hike it back three miles," one of the friends said.

"You boys don't have to hike it back. There are a couple of rooms above the bar if you want to crash here," the bartender said.

"Oh I don't know if we should."

"Of course you should. I'll be closing this place down around 3. That is only a few more hours. Hang tight in here. The next round is on me. Don't worry about walking all the way back," he said while pouring the friends some more beer.

"Man, this guy is a class act," the friend said.

"Appalachian hospitality. We would never get this treatment back home in the city," the other said.

The bartender brings them a fresh beer a piece and the four raise their glasses in unison.

"To you Joe. Best bartender in Appalachia!" they shout.

"Thank ya boys. But let's get one thing straight. It's Appalachia. Kind of like I'm gonna throw an apple at cha," he said laughing.

The friends take turns correctly pronouncing the word Appalachia.

Another couple of hours pass and nearly everyone is now gone from the bar.

"Alright fellas, the room is all set upstairs. Ya'll can go on up. I'll be up in little bit after locking up."

The four friends stumble their way towards a back entrance where they see a large rusted metal door that says EXIT above the frame. They open the door and walk outside where they see some old wooden steps leading up to a balcony. They all head up the steps single file.

Upstairs, there is a large wooden door that appears to have been freshly painted in a barn door red finish. There is a small sign beside the door that says Wolf's Den.

The four friends open the door and enter the room.

"Good Lord, what is that smell?"

The group looks around the room in confusion and disgust. The small space is filthy. There are two old mattresses on the floor with dirty blankets on them. A repugnant odor fills the room as one of the friends begins coughing.

One of the friends notices some old rusted shackles laying on the floor. There is also a set of chains near a mattress that appears to be bolted to the ground.

"What the heck is that!" one of the friends screams.

The others look in horror as they see a small table in the center of the room with three human skulls on it. All around the table, on the floor, is an odd white powdery substance. The powder then trails off towards another door in the back of the room that has a giant wooden board across it. There is blood all around the base of the door.

"What is this place?"

"We need to get out of here. This isn't right!"

All at once, the group can hear doors being locked tightly. They look around trying to find another way out but there isn't one.

Suddenly, a piece of the floor is thrown up and into the air. A head pops up from the hole. It is the bartender.

He pulls his body up through the hole and leaps onto the floor.

"Hey fellas. How ya'll like the room. Cozy, aint it"

"Yeah, this place is a dump man. And it's weird. We're just gonna hike it back to basecamp. Thanks for the invite though," one of the friends says in a nervous voice.

"Well wait just a second, now. Ya'll can't go leaving in a hurry. I brought some more beer for ya," the bartender says with a slight grin.

"Nah man, keep the beer. We're out," the friend says sternly.

The bartender is quiet. He walks slowly over to the back door that has a wooden board across it.

He lifts the board up and tosses it on the floor. He slowly opens the door.

In walks three strange men. The friends don't recognize them from the bar.

All three men are large in stature. The all look older than 55 and appear to be covered in dirt and filth. Their clothes are tattered and torn.

"You boys ain't going nowhere," one of the men says laughing.

"What is going on here? What are you all doing?" one of the friends asks sobbing. "It's feedin time fellas," the bartender says chuckling.

The group of friends stand there in absolute terror as the first stranger steps forward and begins convulsing violently. He falls on his knees yelling and screaming as if he is in unbearable pain.

He starts ripping his shirt off. His back and shoulders begin contorting and growing larger and larger. Massive amounts of hair begin covering his bare skin. His head starts ballooning out and taking the shape of some type of animal with enlarged ears.

Terrified beyond all belief, two of the friends, try to run but one of the strange men blocks their path. Suddenly, the man also begins violently contorting and shape shifting.

A third friend is screaming. As the chaos plays out, the bartender just stands there laughing maniacally.

The first stranger rises off of the ground, completely changed into a werewolf. He stands taller than 6'4 with giant fangs and large hands equipped with razor sharp talons. The animal lets out a horrendous loud howl.

The friends begin panicking; desperately trying to get out of the room.

All at once, the other two men rise up as werewolves. Both are equally tall and fearsome. And both are snarling viciously.

The four friends gather close and cower in fear near one of the walls next to the entrance door.

The three werewolves slowly walk up to them as if to corner their prey. With teeth snarling, and claws protruding, they lunge at the innocent friends.

Roughly six weeks pass. Summer has turned to early autumn. One day a young recently married couple, who is on vacation to Myrtle Beach, decide to make a detour to Wyoming County.

The man and woman heard about a place called The Rusty Shackles.

23

THE CAVE THING

Miranda and Jennifer were best friends. They had grown up together in a little southeastern Kentucky town about 25 miles outside of Carter County. Now in their twenties, the girls were entering their final year of college at Morehead State University.

Ever since they were young kids, the inseparable pair had a love for the outdoors; especially rock climbing and cave exploration.

Each summer they would make the short drive down the road to explore the caves nestled on nearly 2,000 acres. As the years went, the girls got so good at their skill, they even assisted local first responders when tourists got lost or a pet needed rescued in the caves.

One early August the girls decided to head out for a last minute weekend trip before the semester started.

After making their usual protein snack and beverage run, they packed all of their gear and headed into the cave's entrance.

Roughly 200 yards in--Miranda heard a distress call on her radio.

"Hello, is there anybody out there? If you can hear this, please help. We are lost in the caves. Please help, my dad is hurt pretty bad," the voice said.

"Oh no. We better try and get them help," Miranda said concerned.

"But the offices are closed and you know the 9-1-1 response time here is really bad. Maybe we should try and find them," Jennifer said.

After a brief pause, the girls looked at each and knew what had to be done.

"Can you tell us how far you went into the caves? Can you describe something around you that is weird or would standout? Asked Jennifer.

Silence.

"Hello, are you still there. We are in the caves and want to come and help you out," Miranda said reassuringly.

After a few seconds, the radio crackled.

"Yeah, we are here. Sorry, I was helping my dad. I'm not sure where we are. We only have one flashlight and it's so dark," the young girl said in a quiver.

"Point your flashlight all around. Look towards the sky and along the walls. Do you see anything odd? Jennifer instructed.

Silence.

Miranda and Jennifer take a brief break from their descent.

"This isn't good. We just don't know how far down they are. I wonder what happened to the girl's father, "Jennifer said concerned.

108

"Yeah, let's hope it isn't a bad break or something," Miranda replied.

After a moment, the girl comes back on the radio.

"I found something!" she says with excitement.

"Yeah, I see a large formation that looks like a top hat. It's really round and there is a pointy thing coming out almost like an ice cream cone," the girl explains.

"Oh my, I know where they are!" Jessica yells.

"They are near McCoy Point," she continues.

The girls, now with full confidence, begin their descent deep into the caves.

The girls have gone for what seems like a mile into the deep dark pits of the cave network. There is no light and hardly any sound. All they can hear is the occasional drip of water from runoff hitting the walls.

They stop momentarily and try the radio.

"Hello. Hello. Are you still there? Miranda asked.

Silence.

They keep descending further and further until the air is cold and damp. It is practically pitch dark now. All the girls have for light, is there headlamps.

"I hope you brought extra batteries," Jessica said.

"Wait, did you hear that? Miranda asked.

The faint sound of tapping can be heard.

"I hear it. It sounds like someone is using a tool or something to tap on the cave walls," Jessica said.

They girls try the radio once more.

"Hello. Hello. Are you still there little girl? Miranda asked.

The radio just cracks and pops with static.

"There it is!" Jessica yells.

They point their headlamps up and to the right. A large structure can be seen that looks like a top hat with an ice cream cone pointing out.

"We made it. We are at McCoy Point," Jessica says excited.

The girls begin yelling loudly.

"HELLO. HELLO. WE ARE HERE TO RESCUE YOU!"

After yelling for a while, the radio comes on crackling. Some giggling can be heard.

"Is that you little girl. Are you here,? Miranda asked.

"We are here to save you," Jessica proclaimed.

After a few seconds, the giggling stops. The girls hear a loud thud nearby. They look around with their headlamps but see nothing. It is pitch black and quiet.

All at once, a loud thud is heard again. This time, it sounds like it is very close. Maybe a few feet away.

"Who is that? Jessica asks nervously.

The girls hear giggling again.

Miranda turns and her headlamp beams straight towards the area where the giggling is coming from. She scans up the wall with her light.

AHHHHHHHHHH!

Both girls scream in horror.

Hanging off of the wall is a giant opossum. It must be 20 feet length. Its huge mouth is open revealing razor sharp teeth dripping with blood and what appears to be human flesh. The opossum scurries along the wall towards the girls. All they can do is scream. The rodent stops right in front of them and opens its mouth.

"Help me. My dad is hurt really bad. We are stuck down here," the opossum says with a laugh.

It lunges towards the screaming girls.

Nearly one year later, local, state and federal authorities finally gave up searching for the girls. No bodies were ever found. No leads and no trace of the girls exist to this day.

A few months later, in the early fall, a group of local first responders had been called out to the caves after a man went missing from a nearby nursing home. Luckily the man was located cold and wet near the entrance of the caves. After the man was found, wrapped in a blanket and put into an ambulance, a distress call came across the radio.

"Hello, hello, is anybody out there? The voice said.

"Yes, this is Jason, I am an EMS worker with Carter County. Do you need help?" he asked.

"Yes, thank God. My best friend and I are stuck down here in the caves. We need help. My friend, I think she is hurt really bad," the girl said.

"Hang on, we will send some folks down to get ya'll out. Don't you worry now. Do you know where you are at?" the EMS worker asked.

"Uh, yeah, it looks like we are close to a large top hat with an ice cream cone sticking out," the girl said, her voice quivering.

24

SOMEONE LIVES
IN THE FOG

There once was a man who lived in a cabin about 10 miles out in the country from the town of Mount Airy, North Carolina. Every evening during the warm months he would walk in the woods for exercise. One early July evening, near dusk, he took his usual walk. About 15 minutes into his stroll, he noticed a weird looking thick fog moving in. It was very green in color. Not wanting to take the chance of losing his direction, the man decided to head home before the fog impaired his surroundings.

As he walked away from the eerie mist, the sky became darker and darker. Dusk turned into night in only a matter of minutes. Luckily the man always carried a flashlight with him whenever he went on walks. So he turned on the flashlight and began shining it around.

Now the fog was all around him.

In fact, he could hardly see a few feet in front of his hands. He tried walking a little faster in order to get home quicker.

However, the fog was so thick, everywhere he shined his light, he saw nothing but green mist.

Confused and walking in circles, the man soon realized his worst nightmare had come true. He was lost.

So he decided to sit down by a tree and wait for the fog to lift. After a few minutes passed, he heard what sounded like somebody trudging through the woods with heavy footsteps.

Snap! Crack! Thud!

The sounds grew louder. His heart began to race because nobody lived that far out in the woods. Eventually, he shrugged off the noises as deer.

A few more minutes passed and the sound was gone. However, the green fog wasn't.

The man was starting to grow scared because he knew he had to get home as it was getting very late and his wife would begin to worry. He got up and began shining his light around to see if he could find a familiar object or recognizable landmark that would guide his footsteps home.

Unfortunately, the fog was too thick to see anything.

He barely made it a few feet when he heard the sounds of whispering. He stopped and called out. "Hello, who is there?"

The whispering continued.

"Who is that? Please help me. I'm afraid I'm lost out here," he said with a tremble in his voice.

The whispering stopped.

The man took a few more steps and the whispering started again.

"Please. Help. Me," he said scared.

"Do not worry," the strange voice whispered. "You are one of us and protected now."

"Wait, what?" he said frightened.

He stopped and shined his light all around but saw nothing but the fog. All at once he felt a hand on his shoulder. He turned around and screamed, dropping the flashlight on the ground.

After several hours had passed, the man's wife began to worry that her husband had never returned. Fearing the worst, she grabbed a flashlight and a small first aid kit and began walking through the woods to find him.

Now there was no fog but it was very late and very dark. She walked and walked, calling out his name.

But he never answered.

After a few more minutes of walking, the woman nearly tripped over what she thought was a large rock. She shined her light down on the ground and saw her husband's flash light laying there.

She began calling his name out even more but no answer ever came.

Suddenly a thick green fog moved into the area. She started fast walking the opposite direction to get away but the fog was too fast for her. The eerie green mist surrounded her entire body. She shined her light around but could not see any further than her own hands.

Frightened, she called out her husband's name over and over.

All at once, a voice whispered, "Don't be afraid, you are protected. You are one of us."

"Larry, oh my God, sweetie, I found you."

She turned to grab her husband and screamed.

Chapter 9

CREEPY HOLLOWS

25

THE PICKETY CEMETERY

The Pickety Cemetery had always been a place of great historical significance in Marlow, Tennessee. It was an old Civil War cemetery, filled with the graves of soldiers who had fought and died in the war. The cemetery was a solemn and eerie place, especially at night. And it was said that on certain nights, the ghosts of the dead soldiers would rise from their graves and wander the grounds.

Despite its reputation, a group of historical preservationists arrived in Marlow one weekend, determined to fix up the cemetery and restore it to its former glory. They were a small group, but they were passionate about their work, and they had come from all over the country to help.

The first night they arrived, they set up camp near the cemetery, eager to get to work in the morning. They cooked their dinner over a fire and told ghost stories late into the night, but eventually retired to their tents, exhausted from their journey.

As the night wore on, strange things started to happen.

The air grew ice cold, and an eerie fog settled over the cemetery. It was like something straight out of a horror movie. A few team members came out of their tents and noticed the fire was completely burned out; it wasn't even smoldering. All at once, several graves began to shake and shudder, and the sound of marching feet could be heard in the distance. The faint sound of drums was heard. This caused the rest of the team to come out of their tents. They looked all around but all they could see was a thick fog of white cloud.

Suddenly, a group of undead Confederate soldiers appeared from the mist. They were dressed in tattered gray uniforms, their eyes glowing with an otherworldly light. They carried muskets and bayonets, and they advanced on the camp with a single-minded purpose. As the soldiers drew closer, several let out a rebel yell so loud it shook the ground.

The team of preservationists were caught off guard, and they scrambled. Some hid anywhere they could while others decided to defend themselves. But the ones that didn't hide were no match for the undead soldiers, who seemed impervious to their attacks. The soldiers hacked and slashed with their bayonets, their faces twisted in rage.

As the night wore on, the battle raged on. Many of the preservationists fought with anything they could find but they were slowly overwhelmed. Some were wounded, and others were killed outright. But they refused to give up, determined to protect themselves and the cemetery at all costs.

Finally, as dawn began to break, the undead soldiers began to retreat. They vanished into the mist, leaving behind the corpses of the fallen. The preservationists that were left, which was only a few, managed to pull themselves together. Why did this happen? Had they disturbed the graves unintentionally? Did the Confederate soldiers think the preservationists were Union soldiers? To this day, nobody knows why the team was attacked.

The Pickety Cemetery remained a place of great historical significance, but it was now also a place of great danger. The preservationists attack had shown that the stories of the undead soldiers rising from their graves were not just rumors. And so the cemetery remained quiet, waiting for the next unsuspecting group of visitors to fall prey to its undead inhabitants.

26
THE PATH

The Appalachian Trail is a place of great beauty and tranquility. It wound its way through dense forests and steep mountain passes, offering hikers a chance to connect with nature and escape the hustle and bustle of everyday life. But not all who wander the trail were there for a peaceful purpose.

One early fall afternoon, a group of hikers decided to take a detour from the main trail and explore a lesser known path that led deep into the woods. They had heard rumors of strange happenings in the area, but they brushed them off as tall tales and set off into the unknown.

As they walked deeper into the woods, the path began to grow narrower and more overgrown. The trees around them seemed to close in, casting the group in deepening shadows. They heard strange whispers on the wind, and their footsteps grew heavy with dread.

Suddenly, the path opened up into a clearing. But it was no ordinary clearing. The air was thick with an oppressive darkness, and the trees surrounding the group were gnarled and twisted, their branches reaching out like long grasping fingers.

In the center of the clearing was a strange archway, made of dark stone and carved with grotesque symbols. The hikers felt drawn to it, as if it were calling out to them. They stepped closer, and suddenly, they were plunged into another dimension.

The world they entered was a place of darkness and evil. The sky was a sickly green, and the ground beneath their feet was made of writhing, blackened vines. In the distance, they could hear the sounds of screams and moans, and they knew that they were not alone.

As they moved forward, they encountered creatures that defied description. They were contorted and malformed, with razor-sharp teeth and white eyes. They attacked the group, seeking to drag them down into the darkness.

But the hikers were not unarmed and were determined to survive. Each hiker had made sure to pack a firearm, knife and plenty of ammo. So, they fought back, firing rounds into the creatures, sending black blood everywhere. One by one, the creatures were being ripped apart from the bullets.

The hikers began to get away, running and stumbling, their hearts pounding with fear and adrenaline.

As they moved deeper into the darkness, they began to see glimpses of something else. A faint light in the distance, a glimmer of hope. They moved towards it, their fear giving way to a desperate hope.

Finally, they emerged from the dark dimension and stumbled back into the clearing. They collapsed onto the ground, gasping for breath and clutching each other tightly. They looked around, and to their relief, they saw that the archway was gone. It was as if the dark dimension had never existed.

One of the hikers pulled out a rosary and began to pray. The others just smiled in relief.

The hikers eventually made their way back to the main trail, shaken but alive. They told their story to anyone who would listen, warning others to stay away from the path in the woods. Local authorities even investigated the woods. Several other paranormal investigative teams did the same.

But no one ever found it.

Some say the path still exists, waiting to swallow up anyone who dare walk it, into the dark dimension.

27

THE GREENBOTTOM SWAMP

There is a swamp in Greenbottom, West Virginia. It has always been a place of mystery. Locals tend to avoid it, fearing the unknown dangers lurking within its murky waters and dense foliage. But for a group of college students, it was a source of scientific curiosity and fascination.

Each year, a team of science majors from Marshall University made the journey to the swamp to study the local bird population. They would set up near the water's edge and spend weekends conducting research, observing the behavior and habits of the feathered creatures that made their homes in the swamp.

One year, however, things took a dark turn. As the students waded through the murky waters, they stumbled upon a strange looking algae. It was bizarre puke green color, and it seemed to pulse and writhe beneath the surface of the water.

Without thinking, the students reached out to touch the algae. As soon as their fingers made contact, however, they knew that something was wrong.

The algae seemed to cling to their skin, and they could feel it spreading throughout their bodies.

At first, they thought it was just an allergic reaction. But soon, they began to experience symptoms that were far more severe. Their skin turned a sickly gray color, and they started to experience excruciating pain as their organs began to fail.

One by one, the students began to succumb to the disease that was ravaging their bodies. They writhed in agony as their flesh turned black and their limbs began to rot. It was if they were slowly becoming living corpses, trapped in a world of pain and suffering.

As the days went on, the swamp grew even more deadly. The algae seemed to be spreading, infecting not only the bodies of the students but also the creatures that lived in the waters. The birds that the students had come to study were dying off in droves, their bodies wracked with disease and decay.

In the end, only a handful of the students managed to survive. They stumbled out of the swamp, weak and sickly, but barely alive.

Marshall University eventually banned any student from entering the swamp at Greenbottom. To this day, locals avoid it like the plague.

Chapter 10

HOLIDAY TERROR

28

THE DARK ELF OF MILLERSBURG

In the peaceful Amish community of Millersburg, Ohio, Christmas was always a time of joy and celebration. Families gathered together, sharing food and gifts and enjoying other's company. But one Christmas, something dark and sinister arrived in their midst.

It came in the form of an evil elf, a creature that had long been the stuff of local legends and folklore. According to the stories, the elf was an ancient and malevolent being, driven by a hunger for chaos and destruction. And now, it had set its sights on the unsuspecting residents of Millersburg.

At first, the elf's presence was subtle.

It would sneak into people's homes at night, stealing small trinkets and ornaments. But soon, its actions became bolder and more dangerous. The elf began to taunt the Amish families, leaving threatening notes and messages for them to find. It would leave small gifts as well, but these were always tainted with a sense of malevolence and darkness.

The community was throw into chaos. No one knew who the elf was or how to stop it. Some of the more superstitious members of the community believed that the creature was a punishment from God, a warning to the Amish to stay true to their faith and resist the temptations of the modern world.

But despite their fear and confusion, the Amish refused to be cowed by the elf's terror. They banded together, determined to defend their community and drive the evil creature away. It was a difficult and dangerous task, but the Amish were up to the challenge. They set traps for the elf, using their knowledge of the land and their resourcefulness to catch the creature off guard.

But it didn't exactly work the first time.

So, the Amish knew that they had to take a different approach if they were going to stop the evil elf from terrorizing their community any longer. They decided to trick the creature by laying another, more advanced trap for it.

The Amish people began to work quickly and carefully, setting up a decoy tree, decorated with ornaments and lights, to lure the elf out of hiding. They waited patiently, watching and listening for any signs of movement in the woods.

As the night drew on, the elf appeared, moving cautiously towards the tree, with its eyes locked on the sparkling decorations. The Amish waited, hidden in the darkness, ready to spring into action.

Suddenly, the elf let out a shrill cry, sensing that something was wrong. It turned to flee, but the Amish were quick to respond. They emerged from the shadows, armed with various farm tools. The elf charged towards the group, moving with supernatural speed and agility. But the Amish were prepared. They overpowered the creature with numbers. The fighting was intense. The elf moved with speed and ferocity that seemed almost inhuman. The Amish and the elf battled for what seemed like hours.

Finally, the elf began to falter. Its movements became slower and less coordinated, and its eyes began to lose their malevolent gleam.

With one final desperate lunge, the elf charged towards the Amish, but it was too late. They had pinned the creature down, finally immobilizing it with a combination of sheer force and quick thinking.

The elf let out one final scream, a sound that echoed through the town, and sent shivers down the spines of all who heard it. And then, with a burst of sudden energy, it vanished into the air, leaving behind only a faint odor of sulfur and decay.

The Amish stood together, panting, sweating and exhausted from the exertions, but also relieved that the threat to their community had been vanquished. They knew that they had faced something truly evil that night, but emerged victorious.

29

ALL HALLOWS EVIL

Father Thomas had been a priest for many years at a parish nestled in the Allegany County, New York region. It is a beautifully scenic area, offering residents the quiet life to worship and raise a family. Each year, the town of Belmont gathers to celebrate Halloween in traditional fashion. But this year was different. Father Thomas had never encountered anything quite like the events of this Halloween Eve.

With a deep breath, Father Thomas stepped inside the church, his heart racing with fear and anticipation. He was only a few hours from Mass and nobody was there but he could hear the faint sounds of whispering and cackles around the church. Knowing it was holy ground, he was terrified at the thought of an evil entity being able to break through.

"Who's there?" he called out, trying to sound brave and confident.

As he made his way through the church, he could hear the sounds becoming louder and louder. They seemed to be coming from the lower level where the classrooms and recreational room were. He slowly walked down the steps towards the sounds. He made his way through a door and stood at the other end of a long and dark hallway. He reached his hand out and tried to feel around on the wall for a light switch. He finally flipped the switch but it didn't work. He flipped it again and still nothing.

Suddenly, at the end of the hallway, a figure appeared before him, its eyes glowing with a supernatural light. It was Father Thomas's worse fear. A demon. He stood there with a hideous face and a stark growl from its throat. Its eyes were all black.

"You have no place here, priest," the demon snarled, its voice cold and menacing. "This is our domain now."

Father Thomas drew his crucifix and held it up, hoping that it would be enough to ward off the demon's attack. But the creature was not easily intimidated.

"You cannot defeat us," it hissed, lunging towards the priest with a clawed hand. The priest moved quickly out of the demons way but fell backwards into a coat rack, knocking it over and making a loud noise. Suddenly, he saw more figures at the end of the hallway. The demon turned towards those figures and began screaming in an unknown language.

All at once, the entire hallway was filled with demons everywhere. It was as if a portal had been opened in the downstairs. Demons were pouring out in droves. Father Thomas was absolutely mortified. He tried to remain calm and vigilant, clutching his crucifix.

Without much time left, Father Thomas gently closed his eyes, took a few slow breathes and began praying, calling on the power of Saint Michael the Archangel to aid him in his fight. And then, with a powerful surge of strength, he struck out at the demon with all his might. The demon let out a scream, its form flickering and wavering in the holy light. The priest could see that his efforts were working, but he knew he would not last long battling the demons alone.

"Saint Michael," he called out, his voice ringing with desperation. "I need your help!"

All at once, a figure appeared beside him, glowing with an intense bright white light. The figure wore armor and was wielding a giant sword and shield. The sword emanated a radiant light that was like a laser beam. It was Saint Michael himself, and he had come to help Father Thomas in his fight.

"Have no fear, Father," Saint Michael said, his voice calming and reassuring. "Together, we will defeat this evil and restore the holy order of light."

Father Thomas could feel the strength and power of the archangel beside him, and he knew that no weapon formed against him would prevail. He knew at that moment that the evil would be defeated. He drew on his faith and the holy powers that he possessed, calling upon the blessings of Christ to aid him in his battle.

Saint Michael, with a booming voice, cried out toward heaven. "Father, give me the strength to do your justice!" Suddenly, he began slashing and smashing his way through the demons. He struck each demon with such a violent force from his sword that the evil entities blew apart. When the demons attacked, the archangel's shield was used as protection. And it protected both Saint Michael and Father Thomas like a giant fortress wall.

The demons shrieked and howled as Father Thomas and Saint Michael fought back with their holy powers. They pushed the creatures back, banishing them to the fiery pits of Hell where they belonged.

Afterwards, still in shock from the event, Father Thomas kneeled down and looked up at Saint Michael. "Thank you for your help, Saint Michael," he said. "I could not have done this without you."

Saint Michael, who towered over the priest, looked down, reached his hand out and helped the priest up. His expression was serious.

"This is not over, Father," he said. "We have won this battle, but the war rages on. Satan and his minions will not rest until they have conquered this world and destroyed all that is good and holy."

Father Thomas nodded, his face grim.

"What can we do to stop them?" he asked.

Saint Michael looked at the priest with piercing eyes. "We must be vigilant, Father," he said. "We must be ready to fight at a moment's notice, and we must never let our guard down. The world will need us again, and we must be ready."

Father Thomas nodded, feeling the weight of the responsibility that lay on his shoulders. "I will do everything in my power to prepare myself and my fellow priests," he said. "We will be ready to fight when the time comes."

Saint Michael placed a hand on Father Thomas' shoulder, his mighty touch reassuring.

"You are not alone in this fight, Father," he said. "I and the other angels will be with you every step of the way, and Christ himself will be by your side. Together, we will defeat the armies of Satan and protect this world from evil."

Father Thomas felt an overwhelming sense of comfort and strength wash over him as he heard these words. He knew that battle ahead would be long and difficult, but he also knew that he was not alone.

"Thank you, Saint Michael," he said. "I will do my best to honor your trust and fight for what is good and right."

Saint Michael grinned. "Go now, Father," he said. Prepare yourself and your community. And always remember your faith."

"I will," the priest replied.

All at once, Saint Michael burst into the air with a mighty wind. Father Thomas just looked in awe. He slowly looked around at the hallway and the downstairs that was nearly ruined from the fighting. As he turned towards the staircase, he noticed several parishioners were standing there weeping.

During Mass, Father Thomas explained what had happened during his homily.

The church and the town would never forget the evil that sought the destruction of them on All Hollow's Eve.

And they would never forget that good won in the end.

30

A THANKSGIVING CARVING

The Turner family was gathered around the table, while the turkey glistened on the kitchen counter. Each family member took turns saying what they were thankful for. The father, Eddie, listened as his wife and children spoke, but his mind was elsewhere. He couldn't shake the feeling that there was something wrong with the turkey.

"Excuse me," Eddie said, interrupting his wife mid-sentence. "I need to check something in the kitchen."

His wife and kids looked at him quizzically as he left the room, but they didn't say anything. They knew better than to question Eddie when he got like this.

In the kitchen, Eddie carefully examined the turkey, running his hands over its smooth skin and probing its insides. He couldn't find anything that looked out of the ordinary, but he knew that something wasn't right.

He returned to the dining room, his demeanor tense.

"Everyone, we can't eat this turkey," he said.

His family looked at him in confusion.

"What are you talking about?" his wife asked. "We've been looking forward to this all week."

Eddie shook his head, his eyes wild.

"This turkey isn't a turkey," he said. "It's an alien being that's been sent to eat us. We can't let it win."

His family exchanged nervous glances as Eddie pulled out a kitchen knife and began to carve the turkey in a frenzy. He hacked at the meat, muttering under his breath and occasionally letting out a maniacal laugh.

As he pulled out chunks of flesh, he began to see strange markings on the meat, markings that he believed were proof of its alien origins. His family watched in horror as he took the chunks of meat and put them into separate containers. He labeled each container with the name of the family member he believed the meat had come from.

"Eddie, what are you doing?" his wife asked, tears streaming down her face.

"We have to eat them, "he said "We have to consume the alien in order to gain its power and protect ourselves." His family tried to reason with him, but he wouldn't listen. They watched in sheer disbelief as he re-cooked the meat and served it to them, each one eating the piece that Eddie had labelled with their name.

The meat tasted strange, almost metallic, but the family ate it anyway, afraid of what Eddie would do if they refused. As they ate, they could feel something changing inside them, a darkness creeping into their minds and bodies.

Days later, the police would find the remains of the family in the house, each one carved up and stuffed into containers like Thanksgiving leftovers. And Eddie, he was never found, his whereabouts a mystery.

Some say he disappeared into the woods, still searching for the alien being that he believed had invaded their home.

Chapter 11

SPIRIT LAIRS

31
BIG TROUBLE IN BENTON

As the team of paranormal investigators gathered their equipment in preparation for their night in the rundown psychiatric hospital, they couldn't help but feel a sense of unease. The hospital, built in the 1800s and abandoned since 1992, was said to be haunted by the spirits of patients who were lobotomized in the name of medicine.

"I don't know about this," said Jenna, the team's lead investigator, as she adjusted her night-vision goggles. "Something feels off about this place."

"Don't worry, Jenna," replied Sam, the team's tech specialist. "We have all the latest equipment. We'll be able to capture some great evidence tonight."

As they entered the hospital, the team's equipment began to light up with activity. EMF readings were off the charts, and EVPs were being captured left and right.

"I'm picking up some strange signals over here, said Will, the team's audio expert, as he adjusted his headphones. "It sounds like someone is whispering in my ear, but I can't make out what they're saying,"

As they continued their investigation, the team began to feel as if they were being watched. Shadows moved across the walls, and footsteps echoed down empty hallways.

"Did you guys hear that?" asked Jake, the team's skeptic, as he looked around nervously. "It sounded like someone was following us."

Suddenly, the team heard a loud, bloodcurdling scream that seemed to come from deep within the hospital.

"What the hell was that?" asked Jenna, her voice shaking.

"I don't know but we need to investigate," said Sam, leading the team towards the source of the scream.

As they made their way through the hospital, they were attacked by spirits of dead patients. The lobotomized beings were twisted and grotesque, their eyes filled with madness and anger.

The team tried to fight back with what they had, using their equipment, trying to fend off the violent spirits. But the spirits were relentless, and the team began to realize that they might not make it out of the hospital alive.

"We need to get out of here now!" shouted Jenna, as she aimed her camera at the approaching spirts.

Out of nowhere, the hospital began to shake and crumble as if the room and hallway they were in were about to collapse. The team made a run for the exit, dodging falling debris and dodging attacks from the spirits.

Just as they thought they were home free, they saw the spirits converge in front of them, blocking their path to safety.

"We're not going to make it," said Sam, as he readied his equipment for one final push.

The team tried to push their way through the entities but were forced back further into the hallway. It was as if a supernatural wall had been constructed. The group made another escape down a staircase. As they ran down the steps, they were dropping some of their gear out of panic.

"My God, the entire building is falling in!" screamed Jake.

The team made their way down another flight of steps and into what appeared a basement. It was pitch black and the team could barely see, let alone feel their way around.

Once there, they could hear more of the building collapsing.

"We're finished!" shouted Jake.

"Stop it, Jake!" snapped Jenna.

The group huddled down on the floor.

Suddenly, all of the rumbling stopped. They looked around and breathed a sigh of relief. The calmness didn't last long. Sam turned his camera on and screamed in horror as he looked through it in the room.

"What is it?" Jenna asked nervously.

Sam handed the camera to Jenna. She looked and screamed as well.

"What the hell is it you two?" yelled Jake.

All of a sudden a dim light came on in a corner of the room. The group could now see what was being seen in the camera. The entire room was full of spirts, standing and staring with menacing eyes.

The group screamed in horror. The light gently faded out.

32

DEAD END DINER

There is a quaint little diner in Spartanburg, South Carolina called "Hometown Grill" that has become a tourist hot spot over the last decade. It's known for a 1950s look and southern charm. It has also become famous for its chargrilled hamburgers and homemade milk shakes. In fact, the restaurant has become famous for its hamburgers, which were made from a secret recipe that the owners, the Johnson family, refused to share.

One night, the local sheriff, received a disturbing call from a resident of the town who had witnessed something odd at the diner. They claimed to have seen the Johnson family carrying large sacks of meat into the diner, and it definitely didn't look like beef.

The sheriff was determined to uncover the truth, so he paid a visit to the diner the following day, posing as a regular customer. He ordered a burger and an Oreo-cookie milkshake. The sheriff began to observe the Johnson family in the kitchen, watching their every move.

As he ate the burger, he realized that there was something off about the taste. It wasn't like any beef he had ever tasted before. The more he thought about it, the more he became convinced that the Johnsons were using human flesh in their burgers.

He went to the local cemetery and discovered that several graves had been dug up. But that wasn't the end of the horror. It appeared that whoever was robbing graves, was chopping up the bodies on site. The sheriff found random body parts scattered about such as toes and fingers and a partially decomposed forearm with the hand still attached. The sheriff knew he needed evidence to prove that the Johnson family was using human flesh in their burgers. And he knew that the grave robbing would not be enough. He also couldn't barge in and accuse the diner owners without any solid proof. He needed to be sure.

He spent the next few days doing some investigating, asking questions around town, and gathering evidence. He visited the cemetery again looking for more clues. The sheriff also checked the records at the funeral home. He discovered the Johnson family had recently purchased a large quantity of embalming fluid.

The sheriff also took samples of the burger meat to the local lab for testing.

The results came back a few days later, and they were shocking. The meal was confirmed to be human flesh. With this evidence in hand, the sheriff was read to make his move. He gathered his team of deputies and headed to the diner. They burst into the kitchen and caught the Johnson family in the middle of preparing their infamous burgers.

The Johnsons were taken into custody, and the sheriff searched the kitchen for more evidence. He found several large sacks filled with chunks of flesh, a meat grinder, and a large container of embalming fluid.

The town was in total shock when they learned of the Johnson family's horrific secret. After the owners were arrested and the truth about the human flesh burgers was revealed, the town was in a state of shock and disgust. People couldn't believe that they had been eating burgers made from human flesh for years. But what was even worse was the fact that many of the townspeople had become very ill from consuming the contaminated meat.

In fact, many were violently sick. It had turned into a nightmare scenario. The bacteria from the human flesh had spread throughout the town. The local hospital was overrun with patients suffering from nausea, projectile vomiting and violent diarrhea. The doctors and nurses were working around the clock to treat the sick, but the situation was rapidly becoming a crisis.

The sheriff knew that he had to act fast to contain the outbreak. He ordered a team of health inspectors to visit every restaurant and food establishment in the town to make sure that they were not serving contaminated meat.

The entire town was on edge. People were afraid to eat anything, and many were too sick to leave their homes. The streets were empty, and the only sounds were the wails of the sick and the frantic chatter of the health inspectors.

Finally, after nearly a week of chaos and uncertainty, the outbreak began to subside. The health inspectors had successfully contained the spread of the bacteria, and the sick began to recover. However, the town was left with a deep scar, one that would never truly heal.

The Johnson family was put on trial for their crimes, and the evidence was overwhelming. They were found guilty of multiple counts of grave desecration and cannibalism and were sentenced to life in prison.

The town tried to move on from the nightmare that had consumed it, but the memory of the human flesh burgers lingered. It became a dark legend, a story that parents told their children to warn them about the dangers of secrets and hidden truths.

And for the rest of their lives, the townspeople would never forget the horror and would never put a hamburger near their mouths again.

33

FUNERAL PARLOR PRANK

There were two teenagers, Sam and Jess, who spent their weekends prank calling funeral homes. They loved hearing the different reactions they would get from the funeral directors, and they would always compete to see who could come up with the creepiest prank.

The teens never saw any harm in the calls, and never went too far with the prank.

One Friday afternoon, they decided to up the ante and target a funeral home in a nearby town that had a reputation for being haunted. They giggled with excitement as they dialed the number and waited for the owner to pick up.

"Hello, this is Smith Funeral Home, how may I assist you?" the voice on the other end answered.

"Um, hi. Is this where they keep the dead bodies?" Sam asked, trying to sound as creepy as possible.

The owner sighed, clearly annoyed. "No, this is a funeral home. We provide dignified services for those who have passed away. Please do not call here again."

Sam and Jess erupted with laughter at their success. They fist bumped each other and then decided to wait a while and give it one more try.

They passed time eating pizza and coming up with an elaborate story. They also installed a voice changer app on their smart phone to assist them. They selected a voice that was that of an adult man.

This time Jess made the call.

"Hello, this is Smith Funeral Home, how may I assist you?"

There was silence.

"Hello?" the voice asked.

Suddenly the sound of a weeping man came on the line.

"This is Smith Funeral Home, right?" the man asked.

"Yes, how may I help you?" the voice asked.

"You all had my father's viewing there last month." I'll never get over what you all did."

"Sir, what are you talking about?" the voice asked. "Which viewing are you referring to?"

"You know damn well which one," the man said angrily. "The one where we found my father's body with the head missing,"

"Excuse me, what?" the voice asked anxiously. "Sir, you are mistaken. You have the wrong funeral home. We would never...."

The man on the other line interrupted the funeral home owner.

"Don't you call me a liar?" My father's head was severed and it is all your fault. You're going to pay for this. And the whole town will know what you are doing!"

Jess hung up the phone and the teens laughed hysterically.

Just then, her phone rang.

"Oh crap, what if it's the funeral home guy?" Sam asked.

"It can't be, I used a call block," Jess said.

"Well what does the number say?" Sam asked nervously.

"It just says unknown," Jess said, calmly.

She declined the call. However, a few minutes later her phone rang again. Same unknown number. She declined the call again. This went on a few more times, before Jess finally silenced her phone.

Eventually the calls stopped. The girls decided to put binge watch a Netflix show to take their minds off of the earlier events.

Suddenly a loud banging was heard. The girls jumped up and screamed. It sounded as if someone was using their fists to pound on the front door.

"Oh my God, who would that be?" Sam asked.

"I have no clue but that scared the crap out of me," Jess said, her heart racing.

"Oh, no, you don't think it's that funeral home guy?" Sam asked, nervously.

"Are you kidding me? How would he know where I live?"

Jess gets up and goes to the door. She looks out of the window and doesn't see anywhere there. She slowly opens the door and nobody is there.

"Stupid neighborhood kids," she mumbled. She closes the door and goes back to the couch.

Roughly three minutes later, a loud banging is heard.

"Jess, don't go to the door!" screams Sam. "Let's just call the police."

"It's somebody just messing with us," Jess replied confidently. "Don't be so scared."

Jess runs to the door and flings it open. She screams in horror as a tall, bizarre looking man in a cheap velvet suit is standing there. He is wearing a crazy looking top hat. His look and clothing style resemble a mid-century gothic undertaker.

"Why would you call my funeral home?" he said with a robotic voice.

"I'm calling the cops, you psycho!" screamed Jess.

She slammed the door in the stranger's face. She pulled her phone and dialed 9-1-1.

"This is 9-11."

"Hello, yes, my name is Jessica, there is a strange man at my door harassing me. I live at 104 Terrace Avenue.....'

"Ma'am. Ma'am.

The cell phone signal started fading. And the call was beginning to drop off. Just then a weird voice came on the line.

"Ma'am. Hahahahah. You never should have called my funeral home," the voice said.

"Oh my God, no!" Jess screamed, dropping her phone on the floor. This prompted Sam to jump off of the couch.

"Jess, what is it?" Sam asked whimpering.

"The man from the funeral home, was just on my phone. But how? I called 9-11," she said.

"This is just a sick joke, "Sam said. "Come on, I'm getting my car keys, we are leaving. We'll sneak out the back,"

All at once the front door explodes off the hinges. The girls scream in terror.

"THE HELL YOU WILL," YOU ARE MINE FOREVER!" screams the man.

The girls run to the back of the house where the back door is. They swing it open and find the man standing there. They scream and slam the door shut. They run upstairs, pull the attic ladder down, and climb up. Both girls are crying.

"Shhhh, he will hear us. We'll be safe up here. We have to be quiet," whispered Jess.

They hear the downstairs back door blast open. The sounds of the house being torn apart can be heard.

Suddenly, everything goes quiet. A few minutes pass.

"Do you think he is gone?" asks Sam frightened.

'I'm not sure, let's wait a while before we go down. Maybe we can wait until dad gets home," Jess says.

"What if the man is still down there hiding?" Sam asks.

"Don't worry, if he is, my dad will beat his ass," says Jess.

Both girls sit quietly for a few more minutes.

"Did you hear that?" Sam asks.

"Hear what? Jess asks.

The girls are quiet.

Suddenly, they hear what sounds like a creak on the floor boards in the attic near them. They begin to shiver and whimper in fear. The creaky sound happens again.

"I'm scared, Jess,' whimpers Sam.

The creaking on the floor gets closer and closer. It is now right behind the girls.

Jess pulls out her cell phone. Her hand is trembling so hard from fear she can barely get the flashlight feature to work.

She slowly turns around with the phone light.

"YOU'RE ALL MINE!" the man screams.

The girl's screams can be heard from outside the home.

Chapter 12

UNEXPLAINED MYSTERIES

34

THE COFFIN IN THE CREEK

Growing up in Lavalette, West Virginia did not present the life of constant entertainment. But if you were a kid and loved the outdoors, it was the place for you. And for two teens, Matthew and Courtland, every weekend was a new adventure exploring.

One weekend during the summer, the boys decided to make a pizza run. Every week, they would walk the tracks to pick up pizza. And this weekend was no different. But the boys decided to make a pit stop beforehand after learning about an old train car that was found in a nearby creek bed.

As the boys waded through the murky waters of the creek, their flashlights barely illuminating the path ahead, they heard an eerie sound.

"What the heck was that?" whispered Matthew.

"I don't know, but let's keep moving," replied Courtland, his heart pounding in his chest.

As they made their way upstream, they stumbled upon an old, rusted train car, half submerged in the water. The boys cautiously approached the car, their curiosity piqued.

"Check this out, Matthew!" exclaimed Courtland. "It's like something out of a horror movie."

Suddenly, they heard a low growling noise and the train car shook violently. The boys froze, their hearts racing.

"What was that?" asked Matthew, his voice trembling.

"We need to get out of here," replied Courtland, his eyes scanning the dark surroundings.

As they turned to leave, they saw a figure emerge from the water. It was a man, but not like any man they had ever seen before. He was covered in mud and debris, his hair was long like dirty shoelaces, and he had a twisted grin on his face.

"Run!" shouted Matthew, as they darted down the creek.

But the man was fast, and soon caught up to them. They could hear his ragged breathing and feel his cold breath on their necks.

"What do we do?" asked Courtland, panting heavily.

"Keep running!" replied Matthew, his heart pounding in his chest.

Just then, they spotted a wooden crate by the side of the creek. Part of the box was submerged in a muddy pit of water. Without hesitation, they climbed inside and pulled the lid closed behind them.

They could hear the man snarling outside, trying to claw his way into the coffin. But the boys held firm, their bodies trembling with fear.

"Keep holding the lid down!" yelled Courtland.

"I can't hold it much longer," replied Matthew.

Finally, after what felt like an eternity, the man slunk back into the water and disappeared from sight.

The boys waited for what seemed like hours, until the sun began to rise and they felt safe enough to emerge from the coffin. As they walked back to their homes, they knew they had experienced something so bizarre, it would be hard to believe.

But such is a kid's life around those parts.

35
THE BEECH FORK UFO

The skies were clear that summer evening, and the father and son were excited to launch their model rocket into the air. This had become an annual summertime tradition for the two. They had done this many times before, but tonight felt different.

As they arrived at Beech Fork State Park, they couldn't help but notice the eerie silence that surrounded them. It was as if the forest and land had held its breath in anticipation of what was to come.

The father and son quickly set up their rocket and prepared for liftoff. They had just counted down when something strange caught their eye. A massive object was descending from the sky, slowly but surely making its way down towards them. The object was like nothing they had ever seen before; it was enormous, circular, and shone with a bright light.

They watched in shock as the object landed on the ground, creating a loud and thunderous noise. The father and son stared at each other in disbelief, unsure of what to do next.

They had never believed in aliens or UFO, but here they were, face to face with one.

As they stood there, frozen in fear, the UFO began to open, revealing a blinding white light. The father and son were both sucked in the light and lifted off the ground, taken into the unknown reaches of the universe. As they traveled, they could feel their bodies changing. Something was happening to them beyond their comprehension. The father and son watched in terror as their skin began to stretch, their bones started to twist and contort in unnatural ways. It was as if they were being reassembled into something entirely different.

Finally, they arrived at their destination. They were no longer father and son but creatures beyond human understanding. They had been transformed into something unrecognizable, something far beyond human existence.

The father and son were now a part of the universe, and their human form was gone forever.

They would never return to planet Earth, much less to Beech Fork State Park again.

36

The Georgia Lake Creature

It was a typical summer day in rural Appalachia Georgia, the air hot and humid, the sky a clear blue. The lake was peaceful, with small ripples gently lapping at the shore. In years past, this particular lake would be packed with families and boats during the summer. It would be busy with swimming, fishing, barbequing and Fourth of July celebrations.

But this year was much different. The lake was practically desolate.

Beginning roughly three years ago, boats started disappearing without explanation. Then, people started going missing. Fisherman would never return home. Local authorities brought in state and federal investigators. But the missing persons were never solved.

The lake had become a source of fear and superstition among the community.

A group of scientists arrived in town, determined to solve the mystery of the missing boats and fisherman. They set up their equipment and began their research, scanning the depths of the lake.

But they found nothing. As the day turned into dusk, the team packed up their gear and headed back to their RV for the night.

That's when things took a turn for the worse.

The lake became alive with movement. The water churned and splashed, and the scientists could hear a deafening rumble that seemed to come from deep within the lake. They quickly realized that there might be some sort of creature at the bottom of the lake. Maybe they had disturbed its slumber. Whatever it was, it sounded huge.

Then, all at once, the water turned into waves. The creature began to surface. It's massive, scaly body broke through the water's surface. It looked like a cross between a sea kraken and a giant small mouth bass. It was some sort of mutant. It appeared to have razor sharp teeth and massive claws. The scientists knew they were in deep trouble. They tried to run but the creature made landfall. It had giant legs and webbed feet. In an instant, several scientists were snatched up and crushed within its massive jaws. The rest of the group scattered in panic, taking shelter and hiding wherever they could.

One of the scientists was hiding in the main marina boat house and rental store. He could hear the creature outside tearing apart some of his teammates. All at once, he heard something in the boat house. He crawled around on the floor to find somewhere safer to hide. He made his way towards the back of the shop when he caught something out of the corner of his eye. It was somebody else hiding. He made his way over to the person.

It was a college-aged student who works there during the summer, renting boats and fishing supplies to the locals.

The student told the scientist that he was aware there was a creature in the water. And that this confirms all of the rumors. The scientist explained to the student that the creature was massive and killing and destroying everything in its path. The student paused and thought for a minute. Then he thought of a plan.

He explained to the scientist how many, many years ago a group of fisherman used to sneak out on the lake and use dynamite for fishing. One day, a boat full of chemicals was accidentally blown up and sunk, causing the lake to be closed to the public for over a year. The scientist told the student that this creature might be the result of toxic chemicals leaked into the water and food supply for the fish and wildlife.

Nevertheless, the two had to come up with a plan and quick. The creature was tearing boats apart and eating more scientists.

That is when the scientist had an idea. He wanted to know where the fisherman kept all of the dynamite. The student explained that it was in an old un-used building near the lake shore. So the two came up with a plan to get all of the dynamite, load it on a pontoon boat and ram the creature, hoping it will blow up. The scientist told the student to run and grab the dynamite while he distracted the creature.

So the scientist took off running out of the store, screaming and waving his arms like a madman. The creature caught site of this and began chasing him. Amid the distraction, the college student ran into the old building and found a pile of dynamite. He grabbed it all and shoved it into a worn out and tattered sack.

The plan was working.

The scientist made his way back to the boathouse. The creature was right on his heels. The student climbed on a pontoon and boat fired up the engine. He slowly pulled out onto the water. The scientist took one giant leap onto the back of the boat just as the creature reached out to attack.

The pair made their way out onto the water, waiting for the creature to come after them. They could see it slither its way into the lake and disappear under the murky waters.

Suddenly, it emerged out of the water like an atomic bomb. It roared and sent a giant wave across the boat, nearly capsizing it. The student was launched completely out of the boat and into the water like a missile. The scientist was thrown so hard against the railing of the boat that it nearly killed him. Beaten, bloody and weak, the scientist grabbed a hold of the boat's railing and lifted himself up. He held up the satchel of dynamite. He then reached into his pocket and pulled out a zippo lighter.

The creature roared and swung its claws at the boat, ripping a chunk out of the side. He swung again and ripped most of the canopy off. The scientist let out a yell to keep the creature fixated on him.

Meanwhile, the college student was able to surface out of the water, a few hundred yards away. He watched in disbelief as the creature tore the boat to shreds.

Just as the creature was readying for another attack, the scientist lit a stick of dynamite and dropped it into the bag. He took off running and leaped directly into the creature's mouth.

The dynamite exploded so violently, it could be seen and heard several miles away. The explosion was so forceful, it blew the creature into a million pieces along with boat and the scientist. The college student watched the explosion from the shore, soaking wet and barely able to catch a breath.

After the smoke cleared and water settled down, the student hung his head in sadness knowing the scientist had sacrificed himself for him. But he also knew, that because of the scientist's bravery, the lake would be a normal place again. Families, children, and fisherman could once again enjoy the town's biggest attraction.

Chapter 13

TREACHEROUS TOWNS

37

THE CULT OF KNOXVILLE

A historic football town in Appalachia. Knoxville, Tennessee attracts tourists from all over and every weekend during the fall, its largest stadium is packed. But many years ago, time stood still. It was during the malt shops and poodle dress era. The year was 1956. And the town had been looking to build on a good football season after finishing last year with six wins. But sadly, this year football would be on hold.

Rumors had been swirling for months about a ritualistic pagan cult on the outskirts of the city. Strange demonic looking artifacts and symbols had been left around the area in prominent places. At first, the locals thought it was a prank. But after several people were found murdered with the same symbols connected to their bodies, the worry and fear began to set in.

In the last week, a famous family known for their philanthropy and their restaurants all across the state, went missing. The police had no leads. The only evidence found was a drawing of a pentagram with a goat's head in the middle that was left in the middle of their living room. The drawing appeared to be inked with blood.

Desperate for answers, some of the more courageous townspeople banded together and began patrolling the streets at night, hoping to find one of the cult members.

As they walked throughout town, the group discussed some of the strange practices of the pagans.

"I heard they worship trees," one man said.

"Not trees, they worship the devil," another group member proclaimed. "Just look at all of the evil crap they leave around here."

"Well, whatever they worship, it isn't good and they have to be stopped," said a woman in the group. "This is a good Christian town. We care about people. We have low crime and our families are safe. We have to do something about this evil."

As they continued their patrolling, they stumbled upon a small clearing in the woods, just on the edge of town. They noticed smoke as they moved closer. When they arrived, they could tell a fire had been lit there recently as the wood was still smoldering.

"You think they were here?" one man asked.

The group, armed with shotguns, pistols and hunting rifles, searched the area.

"Hey, check this out over here!" the woman yelled.

They all rushed over to where she stood. The woman pointed down at the ground. What they saw next was disturbing to say the least. It was a large circle of blood in the shape of a star. Next to the symbol was a pile of human remains, mainly intestines and skin.

"This is not from an animal. This is human," one of the men said.

The sight and smell made some of the group members vomit.

Suddenly, they heard what sounded like a large branch snap. The group quickly turned around and saw a large man with a weird looking mask on in the shadows.

"You there, stop!" one of the members yelled. The man took off. The group chased him through the woods for what seemed like a mile. He was fast, almost like a deer.

Finally, the man came to a section of woods and stopped. He turned around and began laughing loudly through the mask.

"Who are you?" the woman asked.

"I am the earth, I am the fire, I am forever," the voice behind the mask proclaimed.

"I don't care what you are. You are going downtown to talk to the cops," one of the men said. He pointed his shotgun at the cult member.

All at once, the masked man stretched his hands out and started chanting. The words grew louder and louder. The trees behind him began to shake.

"What the hell is going on?" the woman asked.

The chanting was incoherent and he would not stop. He just kept getting louder and louder.

Suddenly, a dozen more cult members came running out of the woods behind him. They were all wearing bizarre looking masks. It appeared as though the masks were made of some type of skin and animal fur. They were dressed in torn clothes and were wearing homemade jewelry around their necks. Some of the carried make-shift weapons like clubs made out of tree branches.

The cult members rushed the townsfolk. But as they did, the group opened fire on them with their weapons. Each member of town brought down a cult member easily. After the smoke cleared, the townspeople walked over to the dead cultists who lay scattered all around.

"Oh no, what have we done?" one of the men asked.

"We saved an entire town, is what we did," said another man.

"But we shouldn't have killed them like this. We needed to bring them in," said another.

"They were going to kill us. They had weapons and were coming right at us," the woman proclaimed.

"Well, let's see who these psychopaths really are," said one of the men. He reached down and pulled one of the cult member's masks off. He jumped back in panic from what he saw.

It was the Knoxville Mayor.

"Oh my God, this can't be!" the woman shouted.

One by one, the group started pulling off masks. And each time, revealed another important member of the city. The sheriff, a city councilwoman, a member of the county commission and so on.

"It's the who's who of this whole city and county!" one of the men proclaimed.

To the group's shock, the leaders of Knoxville and Knox County were the cult members and had been covering up this secret for a long time.

Nobody knew why they were doing it but the story made national headlines.

And to this day all of the missing person's cases are still unsolved.

As the years went by the city and the county eventually recovered and were able to get back to normal lives.

But they never forgot the year of the cult.

38

THE LYNCHBURG LIAR

In the quaint city of Lynchburg, Virginia, there lived a reclusive man named George. He wasn't necessarily a strange person but one that most folks didn't get along with. The reason being he was known to everyone as a professional liar.

He would weave tales of all shapes and sizes, from grandiose stories of heroism to small white lies that he believed would get him ahead. He believed his words could move mountains and that he could make anyone believe anything. He truly prided himself as an orator and someone who would be remembered as a mover and shaker.

"George, how was your day?" his wife would ask.

"It was fine," he would say, when in reality, he spent the day at the bar drinking with his buddies.

"Did you pay the bills?" she would ask.

"Of course," he would say, when in reality, he hadn't paid a single one.

His lies were so intricate that he had started to believe them himself. He had convinced himself that he was a wealthy businessman with connections in high places. In reality, he was nothing more than a broke, unemployed man who had been living off of his wife's income for years. He would get up early, get dressed and claim he was going to his job. And every time his wife would question him as to why some of her money was gone in the bank account, he would come up with another elaborate lie.

But one day, his lies caught up with him. He had told his wife that he was going on a business trip to New York, but in reality he was going to travel, with a friend, to Las Vegas to gamble away what little money they had left. His wife found the plane ticket and confronted him.

"George, why did you lie to me?" she asked.

"I didn't lie," he said. "I had to go to New York for business."

"You're lying, George. I found the plane tickets to Las Vegas in your desk drawer," she said.

George was caught in his lie, but he couldn't stop himself. He continued to spin lies to cover up his previous ones. He told his wife that he had to go to Las Vegas to meet with investors who could save their financial situation. She knew it was another lie, but she didn't know how to stop him.

Days turned into weeks, and weeks turned into months. George's lies continued to pile up, and he couldn't keep track of them anymore. He told his friends that he had been in the military and had fought in Iraq, but in reality, he had never left the country. He told some relatives that he had an Ivy League degree that had helped propel him into a high level executive position. In reality, George had never even attended college.

One night, he was out at the bar. He had been telling a group of strangers that he was a famous musician who had toured with some of the biggest names in country music. One of the strangers turned out to be a real musician, who was in town for a show, and he called George out on his lies.

"You're not a musician," the stranger said. "I've never heard of you."

George tried to deny it, but he knew he had been caught. The stranger and his friends began to confront George, and he knew he had to get out of there before things got violent.

He left the bar and started to walk home, but he could feel eyes watching him. He heard whispers in the shadows, and he began to get frightened. As he walked down the dark street, he saw a figure looming in the distance. It looked short and disfigured. As he approached the figure, it became more sinister.

It was clear to George this figure was a demon. Its eyes bright yellow and skin was pale. Its skin was rotten and stretched like laffy taffy.

"I know what you have done, George," the demon said. "I know all your lies."

George tried to run, but he knew it was too late.

The demon was upon him, and he had nowhere to go.

"Please, I will change. I promise," he whimpered.

"You've had your entire life to change. But you chose to make things worse. You have destroyed friendships, your marriage and anyone who has ever gotten close to you," the demon stated.

"But what about redemption?" George asked.

The demon paused as if to search George's mind and soul.

"That's right. I can be redeemed. In fact, I visited my local pastor yesterday about all of this. We talked for a long time. I'm going to get baptized and everything," George said with confidence.

Unfortunately, George was spinning another lie. He never visited with a pastor. In fact, George has spent his entire life denouncing religion, Christianity in particular.

The demon began laughing.

"Why are you laughing?" George asked frightened. "I told you the truth."

You are incapable of telling the truth which makes you a perfect fit for us.

Suddenly the ground opened and the demon pushed George into a pit.

Days went by and nobody knew what happened to George, not even his wife.

Local authorities had no clue as to George's whereabouts. His wife questioned everyone she could think of in town.

One afternoon, a knock was heard on her front door. She opened the door to find an old elderly woman standing there.

"Are you George's wife?" the old woman asked.

"Yes, I am. Have you seen him or know him?" George's wife asked.

"I didn't know your husband but I know what happened to him," the woman said.

"What happened to him?" his wife asked frantic.

"I was walking home and saw him talking to himself from across the street. I thought he was just another drunk man. He kept talking loudly and started arguing. But nobody was with him. Then all at once, the ground split open and he fell into a hole. I nearly had a heart attack," the woman said with seriousness.

George's wife paused and then began laughing.

"Why are you laughing about something this serious?" the old woman asked shocked.

"Lady, did my husband put you up to this?" George's wife asked.

"Of course not, I told you I didn't even know him," the woman said frustrated.

"You are lying. This never happened. You and George are both liars," George's wife said.

She slammed the door shut.

39

HALLOWEEN TOWN
OF HARRISBURG

It was a few hours before the night of the annual Halloween festival in Harrisburg, Pa. The city streets were lined with spooky decorations. Many of the local businesses had closed early in anticipation of the years biggest even. The town square was already filled with people dressed in costumes and live music could be heard all around. The festivities had always been the highlight of the year for the town.

The town festival organizer, David, had been acting strange for weeks leading up to the event.

As the night drew closer, people began to notice something was not quite right. The usual fun and games had been replaced by an eerie atmosphere, and nobody seemed to be having a good time. The music was playing and the food trucks were busy with customers, but everyone was acting weird this time around.

And unlike every year, David was completely gone from the festival.

Several party goers who knew him, decided to take a look around for their friend. They searched the streets but no David. One of them had an idea to go check out the pumpkin patch. It was a huge field of pumpkins that sat right in town on two acres of land. The local kids loved playing there and it was open to the public for pumpkin picking every fall season.

So the small group of five headed to the patch.

As they got closer, they noticed some candles leading up a patch to a certain section of the patch. They really didn't' think anything was weird about it, considering the whole town was decorated in many ways for this spooky season. So, they continued walking up the path.

As they got closer, they finally saw David.

"Hey, David, what the heck are you doing here? You are missing the entire festival," one of the women asked.

David just stood there with his back turned to the group. It appeared as though he was staring off into space.

"Hey man, everything good?" one of the men asked.

David slowly turned around. He had a bizarre grin on his face. He was holding one of the candles.

"Yes. Everything is wonderful tonight," he said in a very robotic and monotone voice.

"Dude, you sure you are alright?" another woman asked.

"Yes. Everything is wonderful tonight?" he replied again in the same odd voice.

"Uh, ok then. We were just checking on you. You know, it's kind of weird that you aren't at the party at all," another man replied.

"Yes. Everything is wonderful tonight?" David replied robotically.

"Alright man. If this is a prank, it's just stupid. You're standing out alone in a pumpkin patch holding a candle," a man said sternly.

David paused.

"Quiet. Do you hear that?" he asked the group softly.

"Hear what?" a man asked.

"Yeah, I don't hear crap but music and laughing, which is where we need to be right now instead of out here doing nothing. This is boring. Let's split," another woman said.

"Be quiet. And be still. He is coming," David said in a monotone voice.

"Who is coming?" a man asked.

"Better be somebody fun who is bringing some drinks with them," another man said jokingly.

"He is fun. And he will love you all," David replied.

"Who is he?" a woman asked.

"The Pumpkin Overlord," David said.

The group burst out laughing. David's expression didn't change. He was completely emotionless.

"This town will be his tonight," he stated.

"Ok cool man. I think it's safe to say you need to lay off the drugs or booze or whatever the hell you are on," one of the men said.

Suddenly, the ground began to rumble and the pumpkins were shaking so violently, they were rolling around.

"What is that!" one of the men yelled.

"David, come on man. It's an earthquake. We have to get out of here!" a woman screamed.

"Do not move. We must not leave. He is finally here," David said without moving.

Just then a bright light blinded the group. It was coming from the center of the pumpkin patch. The light was so powerful it sent them flying backwards. When they came to they were surrounded by a sea of jack-o-lanterns, each one glowing with ghostly energy.

Then, they saw it. A massive figure looming over them, with a pumpkin for a head and an evil grin carved into its face. The Pumpkin Overlord had been summoned.

The group was frozen with fear as the giant Pumpkin moved throughout the patch.

"Yes, master. I am here to do your bidding!" yelled David at the Pumpkin Overlord.

The menacing giant orange figure let out an ear deafening laugh. Its arms were green vines that had razor-like needles protruding all up and down them.

"Look, I brought you these humans as a sacrifice!" David screamed among the laughter.

The Pumpkin Overlord looked the group up and down and then at David. It then raised one of its razor sharp vine arms and took a massive swing chopping David's head clear off and sending it splattering against a tree.

The group screamed in horror and took off running. They ran as fast as they could down the street and towards the festival.

When they arrived, they tried to tell as many people as possible about the giant pumpkin that was headed this way. Most of the locals laughed it off and kept partying.

Suddenly an ear piercing roaring laugh burst through the crowd. It was so loud, it exploded the speakers on stage and shattered store windows up and down the main street. The whole town seemed to be frozen from the laugh. They could see the Pumpkin Overlord making his way towards them, swinging his long vine arms wildly. With each swing, came destruction and death.

The Pumpkin Overlord made his way onto Main Street, killing and maiming everyone in his path. He destroyed cars and food trucks, leveling each section of street.

The remaining group members ran down another street for safety. As they were running, a store caught their attention. The sign read, "Big Jim's Military Supplies" and the store appeared to be opened. They raced inside where a man was behind the counter.

"What the hell is going on out there?" the man asked.

"Please help us, there is a giant pumpkin thing killing everyone," one of the men said.

The man chuckled.

"You crazy kids. If ya'll aint buying anything, then be on your way," he said.

"Listen, mister. We aren't making this up. Do you hear what is happening out there?" one of the women asked.

All at once, a massive explosion rocked the building and blew out the windows. A nearby gas station had exploded. The sound of the roaring laughter was heared nearby.

"Dear God," the man said."Ya'll wait here!"

The man ran into the back of the store. A few seconds later he returned with what looked like a grenade launcher.

"What is that thing?" one of the men asked.

"It's an M320 stand-alone 40mm grenade launcher," the man said proudly.

"Here ya go," he said as he gave it to one of the men.

"I can't use this. I don't know how," the man said nervously.

The store owner showed the man how to use the grenade launcher that was already loaded. He left again to the back of the store. A few more seconds past and he came back with another weapon.

"Holy!" one of the women said. "Is this a Terminator weapon?"

"It's an M240L machine gun for tactical combat and getting rid of giant bugs, like this bastard outside," he boasted. "Now, let's rock!"

The store owner grabbed the machine gun and they went outside. They could see the Pumpkin Overlord coming down the street, wiping out cars and fileting people with its vines.

The store owner dropped to his knee and opened fire with the machine gun. The bullets shredded the vines to pieces. The creature let out another ear deafening roar. It blew the store owner backwards and into a car. He was knocked completely unconscious.

The man with the grenade launcher took aim carefully.

"Here goes," he said to himself. He fired a grenade at the body of the Pumpkin Overlord. It missed and blew up a grocery store. The explosion was so violent, it threw the creature into some parked cars.

"Only one round left in this thing," the man said.

He waited until the Pumpkin Overlord regained his footing. The orange creature was almost at the man. He raised one of his vine arms that wasn't injured and started to swing. Just then, the man fired a grenade round directly at the Pumpkin Overlord's head, exploding pumpkin guts all over the street and him. The giant creature, now decapitated, fell to the earth and into several cars smashing them to pieces.

The insanity was finally over.

The remaining group came out and hugged their friend for saving them and the town. What was left of the townspeople slowly came out to see the damage and the dead creature.

From that day forward, the town ended their Halloween celebration out of fear a new Pumpkin Lord may be come again.

40

HILLBILLY HIGHWAY TO THE AFTERLIFE

D uring the 1990s, the part of interstate I-64 that stretched from West Virginia to Charlotte, North Carolina was often referred to as "hillbilly highway" because so many mountaineers headed south looking for work and a better quality of life.

However, not everyone was a fan of driving the fast and furious environment of the busy interstate. So, many people chose the slower and more scenic routes that wound through the North Carolina Mountains.

One weekend, a family of four from Huntington, West Virginia were on their way to Charlotte for a short vacation getaway.

The family of four had been driving for hours on the long stretch of highway, the sun was setting and the only lights around them were the car headlights. They had decided to get off of the interstate in Virginia and take the scenic two-lane highway through North Carolina. They heard rumors about the mysterious stretch of road that was possibly haunted, but shrugged it off as silly folk lore. They were a family of skeptics and simply did not believe in an afterlife, much less ghosts.

Until now.

As they approached the North Carolina Mountains, the road began to twist and turn. Suddenly, the car started to shake as if all four tires were off balance. The car jolted as if they had hit something. But there was nothing on the road. The car spun out of control, and the family found themselves in a strange section of road. In fact, there was no road. All they could see was a soft mist throughout the air. The trees looked deformed.

"What the hell is going on?" the father, Frank, exclaimed.

"I don't know, but we need to get out of here," his wife, Sarah, replied.

"Dad, I'm scared," the son said, his voice cracking.

"Yeah, Dad, where are we gonna go?" the daughter asked fretfully.

As they stepped out of the car, they noticed everything around them was different. The sky was a deep purple, and the air was thick. Suddenly, they heard faint chattering in the distance. It almost sounded like a foreign language. They slowly followed the sound until they came across a group of shadowy figures that had emerged from the darkness.

"Who are you?" Sarah asked, her voice trembling.

"We are the lost souls of this realm," one of the figures replied. "And you are trespassers."

The family realized that they might be in grave danger. They had to find a way out.

"We aren't trespassing," Frank said. "Our car hit something on the highway and we are broke down. We need help."

All at once, the figures disappeared. Scared and confused the family looked around.

"Come on, we have to keep moving," Frank said, determined. "There has to be a way out of here."

They searched for hours, but the realm seemed to go on forever. The shadowy figures continued to follow them. As they walked, they came across a fork in the road. One path led to what seemed like a bright light in the distance, while the other led to a dark abyss.

"We have to choose one," Sarah said, fear in her voice.

"But what if it's the wrong path, mom?" the daughter asked frightened.

Frank hesitated. He knew that they had to make the right choice, or they would be trapped in the realm forever.

They decided to take the path to the light. As they got closer, they saw a figure standing in front of it. It was a hooded figure with a scythe, waiting for them.

"Welcome to crossroads of the dead," the figure said, its voice echoing.

"We just want out of here and back to our home," Frank pleaded.

"You can leave," the figure replied," but one of you must stay behind as payment for trespassing."

The family knew what they had to do. They couldn't leave one of them behind. But they also couldn't stay in the realm forever. They decided to draw straws. Frank felt around the ground and picked up a few loose sticks. The short straw would be the one to stay behind. As they drew the straws, the family held their breath. The shortest straw was drawn by their son.

"I'll stay behind," he said bravely.

"No, son, I won't let you, "the father protested.

But the son was determined. "You guys have to go," he said. "I'll find a way out of here."

"No you won't. You will not stay here. You have a full life ahead of you. I will do it," Frank proclaimed.

"But you said we had to draw straws for it!" the son yelled in anger.

"And I am the head of this family so I make the final decision. Go! Now! All of you!" the father yelled.

The family hugged and cried.

"Please don't dad!" the daughter screamed.

The figured moved slowly towards them.

"Time is running out. One of you stays or all of you stay," it said.

The father gave them one last hug and walked away from the family. He waived at them and stood before the figure. The others began walking towards the light. As they reached it, they found themselves back on the highway, their car waiting for them.

They looked back and saw Frank standing in the distance.

He waved at them. Then the mist disappeared and everything returned to normal.

The family hugged and cried again over the father's decision. They wanted to report the incident but they knew nobody would believe them. How would they explain Frank's disappearance? What would they tell friends or his coworkers? What would they tell the rest of the family?

The only thing they were certain of is they would not have gotten out of that realm had it not been for Frank.

About six months had passed. The family still grieved. But they had slowly come to the realization they would never see Frank again. So, they started attending a local church and began receiving counseling. A couple of months later, the family were baptized.

One night, the family gathered after dinner for their usual prayer before bedtime. Both the son and daughter prayed they would see their dad again. The same prayer they prayed every night for the last couple of months.

As the kids lay in bed, they heard a car outside. It sounded like it was in the driveway. Just then a car door was shut. They shrugged it off and closed their eyes.

Suddenly, a loud knock was heard on the front door. The mother sprang out of bed and ran downstairs. The kids joined her. They looked through the peep hole of the door but didn't see anybody. Sarah slowly opened the door.

"Oh my God, Frank!" she screamed.

"Dad!" the son yelled.

"Daddy, is it really you?" the daughter asked.

Frank stood there with a big smile on his face.

"Yes, sweetheart, it's really me," he said with tears streaming down his face.

The three hugged Frank and would not let go. They all went inside. As they sat on the couch, Frank explained to them how he was able to get out of the realm.

"That figure was death. After you all were able to leave, he told me that the only way out of that realm was through Christ, himself. I explained to him that none of us believed in that kind of stuff. It was then that I knew I would be there forever. He needed to trade a soul so he was going to choose me," the father explained.

"So how did you get out then?" Sarah asked intently.

"You all got me out," he said.

"How did we get you out, dad," the son asked.

"When you all were baptized, death became aware. And when you all prayed for me, he had to turn me loose. So you all saved my life," he said.

The family had been reunited. Shortly thereafter, Frank was baptized and the family moved to the outskirts of Charlotte.

They drove the entire trip on the interstate.

About the Author

Ashley Stinnett is an American actor, writer and filmmaker. Born in Huntington, West Virginia, Ashley began acting in theatre as a child. Since then, he has appeared on television, multiple short and feature films along with numerous commercials.

Ashley currently resides in West Virginia with his wife and three sons.

Made in the USA
Monee, IL
11 October 2023

44318566R00115